THE LEGACY SERIES

Series Titles

Finding the Bones: Stories & A Novella
Nikki Kallio

Self-Defense
Corey Mertes

Where Are Your People From?
James B. De Monte

Sometimes Creek
Steve Fox

The Plagues
Joe Baumann

The Clayfields
Elise Gregory

Kind of Blue
Christopher Chambers

Evangelina Everyday
Dawn Burns

Township
Jamie Lyn Smith

Responsible Adults
Patricia Ann McNair

Great Escapes from Detroit
Joseph O'Malley

Nothing to Lose
Kim Suhr

The Appointed Hour
Susanne Davis

Praise for
Finding the Bones: Stories & A Novella

"With themes of home and homelessness, destruction and humanity, Nikki Kallio delivers a focused and nuanced collection with whimsical and surreal connections to Wisconsin and the Midwest. These are very fine stories."

—Nickolas Butler
author of *Shotgun Lovesongs* and *Godspeed*

"Nikki Kallio sets an extraordinary number of storytelling plates spinning in the air, and brings them all to a satisfying rest. She deftly moves through time and space to illustrate griefs both massive and particular, as well as the impossibility of understanding and loving anything new."

—Rebecca Meacham
author of *Let's Do* and *Morbid Curiosities*

"With astonishing range of form, and yet circling her themes like a bird of prey, Nikki Kallio presents Midwestern characters, familiar as our neighbors, grappling in startling ways with outer limits of human experiences. Moving seamlessly between spaceships, hoarders' houses and haunted houses, and scenes of a nighttime world overlaid with a virtual experience, Kallio gives us children attempting to uncover family secrets and parents struggling to hold dark truths at bay. Sharp as shovel blades, each story digs, taps, and unearths what it means to be human."

—Jill Stukenberg
author of *News of the Air*

"*Finding the Bones* is a great example of how genre and lit-fic conventions can be blended to make something new—literary techno-Gothic, perhaps?"

—Tom Miller
author of *The Philosophers* series

"*Finding the Bones* is a powerful collection of stories—filled with loss, grief, hope, and wonder. The humanity and truth in these stories will wash over you in a wave of pain, transcendence, and enlightenment. I couldn't put it down."

—Richard Thomas
author of *Spontaneous Human Combustion*
Bram Stoker nominee

"Stunning compassion in every word."

—Sue Burke
author of *Semiosis*

"Nikki Kallio's deft pen carves a delicate rip in our current space-time fabric, beyond which live the ache and familiarity of her engrossing stories' tenderness, discovery, and abandonment. Prepare to be haunted by a parallel future that never was or never can be but yet feels inevitable."

—Steve Fox
author of *Sometimes Creek*

FINDING THE BONES

STORIES & A NOVELLA

NIKKI KALLIO

Cornerstone Press
Stevens Point, Wisconsin

Cornerstone Press, Stevens Point, Wisconsin 54481
Copyright © 2023 Nikki Kallio
www.uwsp.edu/cornerstone

Printed in the United States of America by
Point Print and Design Studio, Stevens Point, Wisconsin

Library of Congress Control Number: 2022948131
ISBN: 979-8-9869663-3-5

Geographical information in "Geography Lesson" cited from *Webster's New Geographical Dictionary*, G. & C. Merriam Company, Springfield, Massachusetts, 1977, previous edition © 1972.

Definitions for the word *Larus* in "The Fledgling" were taken from the following websites:
1. https://www.inaturalist.org/taxa/4343-Larus
2. https://www.merriam-webster.com/dictionary/Larus

This is a work of fiction. Names, characters, businesses, places, events, and incidents are either the products of the author's imagination or used in a fictitious manner. Any resemblance to actual persons, living or dead, or actual events is purely coincidental.

Cornerstone Press titles are produced in courses and internships offered by the Department of English at the University of Wisconsin–Stevens Point.

DIRECTOR & PUBLISHER   EXECUTIVE EDITOR
Dr. Ross K. Tangedal   Jeff Snowbarger

SENIOR EDITORS
Lexie Neeley, Monica Swinick, Kala Buttke

PRESS STAFF
Alyssa Bronk, Grace Dahl, Patrick Fogarty, Angela Green, Cal Henkens, Brett Hill, Ryan Jensen, Julia Kaufman, Hunter Kiesow, Adam King, Amanda Leibham, Maria Scherer, Abbi Wasielewski

To M & D, my first storytellers

Contents

GEOGRAPHY LESSON

He paced down the inner corridor, heading to the place he thought she might be, rolling a piece of sea glass in his hand. Odd, maybe, that he still panicked when she went missing, because she could never really be lost. At least they hadn't left their human instincts behind.

It wasn't the first time he had found her here. She was too smart to be captivated for long in the classroom with the other children—no, she wanted to find her own answers.

"Have you been here the whole time?"

She looked so small, her skinny kid limbs folded on the floor in the adults' library, paging through the old books. The other children preferred to keep themselves occupied with animal films and flying games or pressing their faces against the viewing portals and watching the stars go by. But Fiona was so much like her mother, or the mother she would have had. Maybe it was one of the worst things, that he couldn't satisfy her curiosity.

He thumbed the piece of sea glass, his talisman, his worry stone.

"Don't you want to be on the field trip with the other children?"

"No. I've seen the goats."

"What are you looking at?"

She looked up at him from the old green volume, one of his own that he'd contributed to the library. They had only brought about four thousand printed books, but also had in electronic storage every book that had ever been digitized. He loved the printed books like Fiona's mother had loved them, but every time he saw them, he wondered about the weight and the space and whether they could've brought more people instead. But they needed a history. They needed a history and a culture to bring with them from Earth. Without those things they were flesh and bone and brain matter and excrement.

She showed him the page she was on.

Bergerac: \\\`ber-zhə-,rak\\. Commune, Dordogne dept., SW cen. France, on Dordogne river 25 m. SSW of Périgueux; pop. (1968c) 27,165; wine; 19th cent. Gothic church; captured by English 1345 and fortified; taken by French 1450.

Bergkamen: \\berk-\`käm-ən\\. City, North Rhine-Westpahlia, West Germany, 10 m. NE of Dortmund: pop. (1969e) 43,585; coal mining; chemicals.

* * *

I want a baby, Leah had told him.

They'd gone camping just after the call came, before the public announcement. They decided to go to the ocean. They were standing on a high rocky ridge surrounded by tall pines, and he wished he could remember the scent of those trees. He could remember the way the strong wind barely moved them, but he couldn't smell them anymore. He remembered the misty ocean droplets on his cheekbones, but he couldn't conjure the salty fish smell of the water. It was there that Leah had found the piece of sea glass and pressed it into his palm.

He had held her tighter, feeling suddenly tiny, a molecule in a cavernous maw of unpredictable space.

You're mad, he had said. *You want to watch it burn to death with everyone else?*

An embryo, she said. *We'll send it with the others.*

He remembered how her hair had twisted around his neck in the wind, but he couldn't remember the smell of her hair.

* * *

Bodie Island
Bodinayakkanur
Bodkin Point
Bodø: \\`bō-,dər\\. Seaport, ⊗ of Nordland co. N. Norway, ab. 100 m. SW of Narvik; pop (1970e) 28,545; trade center, shipping point for copper ore and marble; tourist resort with the midnight sun from June 1 to July 12.

"How can the sun shine at midnight?" Fiona asked.

"It depends where you are on the planet," he said.

"You said it's dark at midnight, just like they make it on the ship."

"Not always. That's not always true."

She looked at him as if she was assessing everything he had ever told her, deciding fact by fact whether or not there might be exceptions.

"What is a tourist resort?" she asked.

"It's a place where people visit."

"Are we tourists?"

"No," he said. "We're refugees. We can't go back home."

* * *

They had argued for months about it and finally he agreed. He came to understand that it was Leah's way of keeping herself alive, even if the government wouldn't give her the golden ticket that would save her life.

Golden ticket. *Charlie and the Chocolate Factory*. He would make sure Fiona knew about the book and he would show her the film, the original. How much of what he knew culturally would be passed on to her, to the other children? *Oompa loompa, dippity do. I've got nothing at all to give you.* All of the fragmented references would become nonsensical to them. They would make their own references and inside jokes. Their own proverbs and insults.

Put it where the sun don't shine. No one of Fiona's generation would understand the joke because now it meant put it anywhere.

* * *

Bodrum, a seaport. SW Turkey in Asia.

"What's SW?"

"Southwest."

"What does that mean?"

He pulled up the holographic globe of Earth and it gently rotated over the table. He stopped it and showed her. "You're here. Anywhere. This is north. This is south, east, west. So, southwest. No matter where you are, if you go this way, it's southwest."

"Which direction are we going now?"

"We have a heading. Not a direction."

* * *

He and Leah had planned to go back to that ocean ridge before the meteor struck, if it was safe to travel. They would go there and they would wait for the wall of fire to come and turn them into ash.

But the astrogeologist who they'd chosen over him was diagnosed with terminal cancer five months before departure. When the phone rang, Leah knew before he said anything. She knew he had a place on the ship because she saw the joy in his eyes a millisecond before he masked it.

* * *

Boeotia, an ancient republic.
Boerne, A health resort in Texas.
Boeuf River, 200 miles long.

"How far is two hundred miles?"

"Far, if you walk it. It would take you a couple of weeks, at least."

"I've walked around the whole ship. I've walked from one end to the other and back."

"That's about two miles. You would have to do that a hundred times."

"I probably have."

"Yes, you probably have."

* * *

The government lied about when it was going to hit. They knew if they told the truth, there would be more chaos than there already had been.

* * *

Borobudur *or Du*. Boroboedoer \bōr-ə-bə-`du(ə)r, ,bör-,\. Ruins of a great Buddhist temple, Central Java prov., Indonesia, ab. 10 m S. of Magelang and 18 m. NW of Jogjakarta; about 1000 years old, built of volcanic lava over a hill, with eight galleries of some 1500 exquisite bas-relief carvings and 430 life-size images of Buddha; rediscovered 1835; under government care.

* * *

Leah hadn't wanted to say good-bye. She wanted it to be as if he were leaving for work. He had argued and protested with his superiors and had nearly lost his seat by demanding that they let Leah come along. But the first astrogeologist's wife had Leah's seat, and they wouldn't force her off.

Besides, the astrogeologist's wife was a botanist, and Leah was a poet.

He looked again at all the books they had chosen to preserve and keep precious.

* * *

He spent hours looking at pictures. The ones he brought; the ones others brought. The billions that were uploaded into the central database. Millions of people that no one would ever know. Birthdays and drunken parties and weddings and other moments of Life on Earth. He looked in private, but they played a constant stream of them in the main passageway, a hall of memories. The children ran by without noticing the human wallpaper. He wondered what they would make of it all, when they grew up. In the common room they showed movies, they showed football and soccer games, historical newscasts and documentaries. What they had brought along with them was everything. What they had with them was their only chance to explain what Earth had been.

* * *

They put Leah on the waiting list, moved her to the priority list, but still seven people would have to give up their seats or die before she could get her seat on the ship.

They knew it could happen. It was how he'd gotten his own seat, after all.

* * *

Boscobel \,bäs-kə-`bel\. City, Grant co., SW corner of Wisconsin.

"That's where it hit," Fiona said.

"Yes."

"Why we had to leave."

"Yes."

* * *

People did die. One of the engineers, desperate to get his girlfriend on the ship, murdered a passenger. But they quickly found out who had shot him, and the engineer lost his seat. They gave the two empty seats to the second engineer on the list and her husband.

Another passenger had a heart attack and died, and his wife gave up her seat. They gave the seats to the next two people on the waiting list. There were still five to go.

There were lots of vacancies, in fact, but they were for the children—the ones they hoped would be born. Planned to be born. They wanted to bring lots of embryos in case women had trouble getting pregnant in space. No one had ever tried it, so they didn't know what to expect. But it had to work.

Three more people died in a car crash on their way to flight training.

That left two.

* * *

Do you hate me? The botanist had said. It was months into the flight; they had avoided each other's eyes that long. He saw her only in the science briefings, this widowed wife of the first astrogeologist.

I don't, he told her, but seeing her face caused sparks of something to burn in his brain. If she had stayed behind on a dying earth with her dead husband, then maybe everything that followed could have been avoided.

Don't you think I see him every time I look at you? she asked him. *Don't you think I see him wasting away every time I look at you?*

* * *

Boscobel \,bäs-kə-`bel\. City, Grant co., SW corner of Wisconsin, on Wisconsin river; pop. (1970c) 2510; farm trade center; founding place of the Gideons, society of commercial travelers (1899).

* * *

"What was it like, when it came?" Fiona asked.

"I don't know exactly. I was on the ship by then."

"But you saw it. I heard you talking to mom one night."

"She's not mom. I told you."

"But I grew inside of her."

"She's your surrogate. That's all. I explained about eggs. You came from your own mother's egg. You have a mother. She died on the planet."

"Yes," Fiona sighed. "I know."

He watched her eyes and saw that somewhere between yesterday and today Fiona had changed from a child to something very different from a child. Did anyone ever see it? That exact moment when it happened?

"We were on the opposite side, already in space when it hit," he told her. "But we saw the glow from the fires. We kept in contact with the people on the other side, as long as we were in range. And then we lost contact."

"What did they say?"

He wouldn't tell her that. He wouldn't tell her how the people left behind pleaded for the ship to return, to let them send up just one more shuttle. How the people on the ship pleaded to go back.

"They were afraid," he told her. "People were scared and lots of people died."

She thought about this for a long time, staring at the same page in the geography reference book.

Boscoreale \bäs-kö-rā-äl-ē\. Commune, Napoli prov., Campania, Italy, at foot of S slope of Vesuvius near Pompeii; pop. (1968e) 19,655; important discoveries of antiquities have been made in vicinity.

"Why didn't they build more ships?" Fiona asked.

* * *

A few months before the flight, he tried getting Leah pregnant. Pregnant women were given a few of the places that were reserved for the children. They saved many places for young girls, because once they reached childbearing age they could carry the frozen embryos.

Parents rioted for a chance to give up their only daughters, for a chance to get them on the flight.

* * *

"Where did they keep this ship? Where did it come from?"

"This ship? They built it in orbit."

"So it never touched the earth."

"No."

"Like me."

* * *

Boskoop \bös-,kōp\. Commune, South Holland Prov., Netherlands, 2 m. NW of Gouda; pop (1970e) 11,600; famous for its nurseries of roses and other flowering shrubs.

* * *

There were lots of places on the ship to run around, to explore. It had been built to be child-friendly. The library was for adults, but mature children like Fiona could go in. There were playrooms and classrooms, and the greenhouse room where the food was grown was another kind of learning center, where children could build their own salad farms. The livestock areas were often the most interesting, where the goats were milked and the milk taken to the dairy room where they made cheese. The children liked collecting eggs from the chickens and laughed when the rooster crowed and the little chicks were born. They liked watching the waste get ejected into space.

* * *

Bordø, an island of the Faeroes.

"Like where the pyramids were?"

"Not pharaohs. Faeroes." He spelled it for her. "They're a chain of islands in the north Atlantic Ocean." He showed her on the ephemeral, rotating globe.

"They look so small," Fiona said.

"They were."

"You could get lost in the ocean," she said. "You could get lost at sea."

Yes, he thought. *It happened all the time.*

* * *

He thought about paying someone to kill the couple standing in the way of Leah's seat on the ship. It was easy to get people to do things in the last days — there would be no prison, no consequences. Everyone had always come to the same end but now they were all coming to it at once, no matter who they were, and there was nothing they could do about it, and it unleashed some kind of collective Fuck You to social conventions and law. There were things that people did in the final days that they wouldn't have imagined doing in normal times.

He thought about it. He went so far as to make casual inquiries in an anonymous part of the city.

But there were still consequences for people who had seats on the ship. If only he could be sure no one would trace the murders to him.

* * *

"How long is a hundred years?"

"Long."

"Will you live another hundred years?"

"No."

"Will I?"

"I don't know."

"Will I see the new planet?"

"Your children will."

* * *

The botanist offered to carry the embryo that would become Fiona. He was ready to have a child three years into the flight, when his sorrow and guilt over Leah's death had subsided enough that he could stand to look into a face that might resemble hers. When he asked the botanist why she wanted to do this, she had said, *It's the closest thing, isn't it?*

* * *

Borstal \börst-öl, `bōrst-\. Village near Rochester, Kent, SE England; site of Borstal reformatory (founded 1902) which pioneered the segregation of young offenders from mature criminals, and other reforms (Borstal system).

Boston Mountains, Ridge in Ozark Plateau in NW Arkansas; highest peak over 2800 ft.

"Tell me again, what is a mountain?"

"Something you climb. And it seems easy when you start but the longer you walk, the taller it seems to get."

Bountiful \\`baŭnt-i-fəl\. City, Davis co. N Utah, 8 mi N of Salt Lake City; pop. (1970c) 27,956; truck gardens; fruit (esp.) cherry orchards.

* * *

When he looked at Fiona now, he saw how selfish he'd been, how selfish they'd all been. He would never tell her what people could turn into because she shouldn't know that. She didn't have to know that. She only needed to live her life and be happy. Maybe he would tell his grandchildren because by then everything that happened would only be a story, a long-ago memory of a time that never was.

* * *

"How many children will I have?"

"I hope a lot."

"Will they remember Earth?"

"No. Only what we tell them."

"We can give them this book. And you can tell them what you remember."

"That's all we can do."

"We don't have a home right now," she said.

"That's right. But we have each other."

"And we have the ship."

"Yes."

"It's taking us home."

* * *

It turned out he didn't have to kill anyone. Other people who were further down on the waiting list murdered people who had seats on the ship. More people got killed, more people were expelled from the ship. It happened so fast and so often that it was hard to keep track of who was going and who was dead. Leah had her seat and so did lots of other new people. Their joy was tempered by the mounting deaths, but they shared a quiet gratitude between them.

And then someone killed Leah to open up another seat.

* * *

Botwood \\`bät-,wŭd\ Town, E Newfoundland, Canada, 160 m. WNW of St. John's; pop (1971p) 4109; has large seaplane base and 30 m. to the E is large airport, western terminus for transatlantic planes.

Bourem or **Burem** \bŭ-`rem\. Town, Mali, W Africa, on Niger river E of Tombouctou.

* * *

Who could he hate? He had contemplated doing to some other husband or wife the very thing Leah had suffered, that he had suffered. The murderer died on the planet, and so had billions of innocent people. Their flesh had burned away from their skeletons, their bones rendered to ash. The clouds that blocked the sun were filled with the dust of the dead.

* * *

"Is anyone left on Earth?"

"I don't think so," he said. "Maybe."

"But it's dark and cold," she said.

"Everything's dying."

"Even the rivers?"

"Yes."

"A river is skinny water and an ocean is wide water."

How could he tell her more and make her understand? How could he make her know what a river really was? He could show her the map, the photographs. But the long grasses that lined the banks, the water bugs, the old fishermen in banged-up duck boats wearing dirty mesh baseball caps waving ancient rods that dripped spidery lines into the muddy water? Fiona had seen grass; they grew it for the goats. But she had never seen tall weeds spiking out of sandy bluffs, she had never felt them scratch her ankles. She had never rolled up her pant legs and waded into shallow streams, trying to scoop minnows into an empty spaghetti sauce jar. She had never tried to see the minnows through the camouflage of sunlight that floated on the tiny ripples made by her feet. She had seen the ocean in the documentaries and had an idea how vast it was, but she would never stand next to one, never know how much she would dwarf, how small she would feel, and incongruously how large she would feel when she danced to the power of the waves.

"That's right. An ocean is wide and a river is skinny."

"Why are you on the ship and not there? Why did you get to come?"

He took a long time to answer.

"Just lucky," he said.

"Am I? Am I lucky?"

SHADOW

Patricia saw the bones poking through the snow before the dog did.

The ribcage caught a grainy piece of black plastic, which fluttered in the frigid breeze, and she stood frozen in the millisecond when her mind tried to process what she was seeing. The partially exposed skeleton waited for her to recognize what it was.

"Hotdog, *no*."

She clipped the dog's leash onto his collar and pulled him close. Hotdog huffed and tugged like Patricia was playing a practical joke.

Last night, unseasonable warmth had melted off some snow, leaving fallen trees and muddy ridges and other things exposed. Then early this morning fog had frozen to the branches, making everything incongruously beautiful and otherworldly—Winterland. But horrible things still happened here.

Oh, Sarah.

If Patricia got closer, she'd know whether or not the bones were human. If she looked closer. That's what she was supposed to do next. That's what people did, because someone should know. But her feet rooted her to iced earth.

Even if the bones weren't human, they'd been deliberately dumped, packaged, and hidden. Didn't the experts all say serial killers practiced first on animals?

She could go back to Bill's truck for the flashlight. The daylight waned and if she could aim a beam at the torn bag, she might get a better look without getting too close. Her phone weighted her pocket—she could call him. He could come and look instead. But she knew what he'd say. He'd berate her for bothering him with this, that she'd got him out of his chair and made him drive her shitty car and what was she thinking anyway?

She could call the sheriff's department. What would she say? That she'd found animal bones in the woods three weeks after deer season? That's all it was; she'd discovered some redneck poachers dumping their illegal take. Couldn't afford tags, or didn't want to bother with them, or just wanted to say Fuck You, government.

Plus, the deputies would want her name, and when they wrote it down on their little notepads, they would look up at her and say it.

You're Sarah Krazynski's sister.

She never talked about Sarah anymore. Not with Bill and certainly not with her son, Peter, who was fifteen now and didn't understand why Patricia hugged him too long before his bus came; why she argued when he wanted to go on the class ski trip with friends.

Just let him go, Bill said, like he'd grown so familiar with the fear in her voice that it had become another marriage.

If these bones were human.

When Sarah disappeared, Patricia's mother had built a shrine at their small home, mounting over the fireplace a 16-inch-by-20-inch painting of Sarah copied from a photograph, done by a friend of the family as a gift, framed free of charge by a local frame shop, also owned by friends of the family. Everyone had become friends of the family. They all wanted a piece of the tragedy, and her mother was all too happy to laminate her pain, keeping it carefully preserved for the world to witness. She used to be Mom, Betty, Mrs. Krazynski, the Avon lady, the Girl Scout troop leader. From the moment of Sarah's disappearance, she became only Sarah Krazynski's mother.

And Patricia was Sarah Krazynski's sister. She became the Other Child, the shadow that leaned against closed doors and tried to hear the muffled voices through the barrier. She longed for her parents to hold her closer, more tightly, but instead it was strangers who pulled her close. *Your poor sister*, they said.

Patricia became popular by default. She was elected to homecoming court in high school only because a sex offender had pulled Sarah into his car, drove her to his shack in the woods, raped her over three days and then bludgeoned her to death. Patricia was invited to parties and bonfires because Sarah had been the second-last victim of the Dairy Farm Killer.

When another girl went missing, Patricia's mother had immediately gone to help the girl's family, who lived thirty miles away. She spent hours with the family, helping with searches, going door-to-door with fliers, organizing benefits and fundraisers. If there was hope for this girl, maybe there was still hope for Sarah.

But then there were the bones.

Sarah had disappeared the first week of school and a deer hunter found her Thanksgiving weekend, her skeleton lined up in the snow next to a frozen creek. She was identified by her dental records.

The ribcage.

Now Patricia's mother lost more than her daughter, she had lost her mission. She withdrew to her bedroom and stayed there most of the time. Patricia's father lost his reason to keep the family together and he left. He called sometimes.

Patricia went away to college in another city where no one knew Sarah's name. She dropped out after a year and a half, after she met Bill, who wanted a quiet existence in another small town that was exactly like Prentice but wasn't Prentice.

What had become of the siblings of the other six victims? Had they been able to forget, move on, live their lives? Did they find a way to hold their families too close and push them away at the same time? Did they ever think about going back to the towns where they'd grown up? Did they imagine riding their bikes on the uneven sidewalks, visiting the street where they'd seen the rust-colored car stop, where they'd witnessed their older sister lean over and talk to someone through the window? Did they try to remember the license plate number years afterward even though they couldn't at the time no matter how many times their parents and police and strangers asked them to try?

Did they sleep?

Did they ever wonder who they would have become if it hadn't happened?

It would snow tonight, according to the TV news. The skeleton and the garbage bag would be covered again and someone else could find it in the spring. It didn't have to be her. If the skeleton was human then some family was already grieving, already lost.

There was nothing she could do about it. Why did it have to be her? She couldn't help. She hadn't been able to help Sarah, or the next girl. She'd let down everyone. She'd seen the license plate and it hadn't helped. She'd possessed in her young mind the combination to a priceless safe, but she had failed, unable to untwist the complex jumble of letters and numbers in the right order.

Patricia turned her back on the bones. She would go back to the truck. She would get in and drive home to their house. She would think about how the siding needed to be replaced, how the back steps needed to be restained next summer. She would think about Hotdog's wet feet and the sound of his nails clicking on the kitchen floor, about washing out the scum around the edge of his metal water bowl. She would think about Bill sitting on the couch watching the game, she would think about calling Peter on his cell phone and asking him when he was coming home.

She would not go back to being Sarah Krazynski's Sister. It was better to be No One.

Someone else would find the bones and they'd have a story to tell for the rest of their lives, nothing more. What would it mean for her, to have to see this, to relive the finality, the frustration, the failure, the loss that went beyond her sister's life?

What would it mean if she walked away?

The dog had stopped pulling on the leash and now looked up at her quizzically.

"I know," Patricia said. "I know."

She took a step toward the tattered garbage bag. The crunch-squeak of boots in snow. She trembled, maybe from the cold. She reached down and pulled away the part of the bag that hid the skull.

Antlers.

Hotdog sniffed at the pieces of bag, looking for remnants of meat. Patricia dropped to her knees. Her body warmed rounded pits in the snow, wet circles soaking into her jeans.

The light began to turn the kind of blue you wait for and think you will never see again.

DISAPPEARING

By the age of eleven, Tommy had grown accustomed to hearing names like *dumbass* and *stupid* hurled in his direction, just because he believed whatever anyone told him, even if it was impossible. But he also knew impossible things happened, ever since he saw that silvery thing land in the field a half-mile from his grandparents' farm, light pouring from round portholes, a strange jaundiced face staring back at him with dark, soulless eyes.

So whenever anyone latched onto his gullibility and told him that the president's motorcade had stopped at the drugstore or that the school principal had won the lottery, Tommy always believed them. He knew what it was like not to be believed. That day in the field he had lost time, hours, waking up staring at a vacant sky, and soon afterward a new kind of abuse followed, names like *looney* and *mental patient*.

As he retreated into his research, determined to understand what he saw, the words began to feel less like stones and more like sand. He worked after school and weekends at his aunt's grocery store, setting out new magazines with Brooke Shields or Madonna on the covers, stocking bags of chips, or sweeping candy wrappers left by small-time thieves while avoiding those who were determined to use his earnestness as entertainment.

"Boy, you're wasting away to nothing," his aunt would say, squishing him against her soft chest, the industrial broom handle crushed between them. "You're so thin, you're transparent."

It was okay with him, if he faded to invisibility.

"You got to stop letting people get the best of you."

He nodded, just so she would let him go.

* * *

When Tommy wasn't at the grocery store, he visited the library, squirreling as many books as he could fit in his torn backpack. Today he had Carl Sagan's *Communicating with Extraterrestrials*, Barlowe's *Guide to Extraterrestrials*, and Donald Keyhoe's *The Flying Saucers are Real*. He'd quickly pack his books, ducking out of the library before Mike from Science Class and his friends saw him and said *Hey, dumbass, don't you know the library's for people who can read?* He would run to the place where no one would bother him, a shady patch along the banks of the Tomorrow River, where he could remain unseen.

"It's getting too cold," his aunt would tell him. "You can't be going out there to the river all the time, you'll catch your death."

Tommy sometimes wondered why the river had been given such a hopeful name in such a dismal town, but maybe its early settlers had arrived with more optimism.

Tomorrow we'll plant corn and we'll have a good harvest. Tomorrow we'll have a picnic and invite the neighbors.

Now it was, *Tomorrow, Mike from Science Class will come into the store and say, Hey, stupid, did you know they cancelled school this week because the sewer line broke and the basement's full of shit? Or Tomorrow, my uncle will find my books and say, What's the matter with you, why don't you act like a normal kid?*

Or maybe *Tomorrow, I'll leave this place and never come back.*

What had happened filled him with confusion, dread, and a sense of heaviness that he could only seem to alleviate by forgoing food. He ate less and less. He'd grown thinner, now convinced that food was only one kind of nourishment. Instead, he devoured words and information and gobbled even the thinnest speculation and theory, searching for clues, building the formula that gave him the best chance of bringing them back. That day a piece of him had been taken, stretched between him and something else like an endless rubbery string, like the psychic tether that forever linked him to his missing mother. If he tried hard enough, perhaps he could reconstruct the formula that brought them here in the first place. He needed to know why the universe had decided that she was different, and most of all, why they had taken her and left him behind.

* * *

"You're reading them books again?" His aunt asked him one day, surprising him out of a trance. He'd been careless, sliding one of his books out in the living room while she puttered in the kitchen. She set a plate of cookies in front of him on the coffee table. "Your momma liked to read."

Tommy knew. Her books lined a bookcase in his room at his aunt and uncle's house, crackling volumes of horse stories and mysteries solved by independent girls. He spent too much time tracing his finger over his mother's delicate signature on the inside covers, flipping through the yellowed pages while he reclined on the sagging twin bed, hiding with a flashlight under the quilt. He devoured the same words she had, seeking clues in the mystery stories she loved.

"Honey, eat a cookie," his aunt said, breaking him out of his thoughts. "Your meds will go down easier."

He closed the extraterrestrial book. He had asked his aunt once, after it happened, if she had ever seen anything strange. She thought about it and finally told him once she'd seen a white deer, but maybe she'd imagined it. When Tommy told his aunt what he'd seen, her face had changed in that way it did whenever she talked about his mother.

Tommy remembered his mother only a little bit, mostly the dark, airless room where his mother slept, curtains drawn, unresponsive when he asked for something to eat. He had one vivid memory of a time she turned on the radio and spun him around the kitchen, singing along to Kim Carnes' "Bette Davis Eyes," her hair dancing. He had other memories, like of his aunt in the grassy driveway arguing with his mother, a green-and-white truck idling. One day he rode in that truck, bouncing on the white vinyl seat between his aunt and uncle, a country music song blaring out the open windows. His mother had to go to the hospital, they told him, but Tommy already knew there were other ways of disappearing.

His aunt held out the plate with the cookie. A pink pill rolled against it.

"I have homework," Tommy said, and put the pill in his mouth but left the cookie, retreating upstairs where he could search through his stack of books in peace.

* * *

The next day Tommy stuffed the extraterrestrial volumes into his backpack along with the black notebook where he kept his carefully gleaned clues. Most sightings, he learned, centered in areas of sparse population, which certainly qualified his town. He wanted to know why certain people were chosen and why others were overlooked, information that seemed to be lacking. He wanted to know whether he and his mother shared any of the same qualities. He didn't really know what they had in common, other than their DNA, but maybe that was enough. If he could find *Them*, maybe he could find her. Maybe he was supposed to be taken with her, and for whatever reason it didn't work, a failed attempt, and he woke up in that field.

Next time, he would get it right.

He slid the three books into the paint-chipped return slot at the library desk where Mae the Librarian worked.

"You looking for more spaceman books, Tommy? I think you read 'em all, but let's see what I can find," she said, standing, aiming herself toward the card catalog.

"Do you remember my mother?"

She paused, mid-step. "I knew her a little, hon. I went to high school with her."

"What do you remember?"

Mae had the same look, the one that his aunt had, like she felt terribly sorry for him. "What do you mean?"

Tommy couldn't articulate what he was looking for. He wished he could see into Mae's mind and sort through her thoughts to pick out exactly the memories he needed.

"I don't know," Tommy said. "I just want to know about her."

Her face relaxed a little. "Well, she was a real sweet lady. She sure loved you. We used to go to the roller rink together in Point, when we were kids, but we sort of lost touch after high school. I'll look for your books, hon."

Tommy left the library, unchaining his bike, his backpack feeling unusually light. He pushed his bike along in the library parking lot, trying to conjure pictures of his mother in his mind, hoping to syphon memories or things she said, but he'd been so young when he was taken from her, or when she was taken from him. He was thinking so hard about her that he didn't notice Mike from Science Class and two of his friends walking behind him.

"Hey, *dumbass*," Mike said. "The library is for people who can read!"

Tommy pushed his bike faster, but Mike grabbed Tommy's backpack, pulling the already torn strap completely away from his body. Tommy's black notebook, pens, random scraps of paper and a bruised, uneaten apple spilled onto the pavement.

"See, no books!" Mike said. His friends laughed. He bent to pick up Tommy's black notebook.

Everything slowed and Tommy's vision sharpened: He saw the creased cover of his notebook, geometric crop circle patterns erased in white, the metal spiral glinting on the gravelly pavement, Mike's scraped, meaty hand closing around it.

Tommy stretched out his hand, but Mike held the notebook out of Tommy's reach.

"Whatcha writing, *dumbass*?" He flipped through the notebook and laughed. "Aliens! Aliens! Are they coming to get you?"

"Give it back."

"Aw, man, look at this!" Mike said, and his two friends obediently closed in around the notebook. "I knew you were crazy—just like your dead mom."

Mike tore a handful of pages out and threw them into the air, then tossed the damaged notebook at Tommy's chest. Tommy failed to catch what remained of his notebook and it landed on his sneakers. He bent to pick it up.

"Maybe you're the reason she killed herself."

Tommy stuffed the notebook back into his torn back-pack and held the bag by its one good strap. He picked up his bike.

Tomorrow, I will be six inches taller and I will break your face.

Mike grabbed the handlebars.

"You gonna cry?" Mike said. "Or you gonna go back to your spaceship?"

If Tommy thought hard enough, he could remember what it was like inside—blinding silver and white, but blurry, with occasionally moving figures he couldn't see, a smell he couldn't identify. Another memory surfaced, a time when he had fallen from a tree and his mother had sped him to the emergency room; it smelled like that, sort of, but cleaner, or sharper, along with a buzzing sense of terror that was both a feeling and a smell. These flashes mainly manifested in his nightmares, leaving him startled awake with a terrifying mixture of relief and loss. He had sensed *they* held an expansive, hidden power that felt unattainable and impossible to understand.

Mike's friends kicked at the few sheets of Tommy's writing that still fluttered at their feet. "Look at him—he's back in space," one said.

"I told you he was looney," Mike scoffed. "Not worth it; let's go."

Tommy dropped his bike and ran for the pages, scooping them up like lost leaves from a dying tree.

* * *

Tommy was more than an hour late for dinner when he pushed open the battered screen door, overwhelmed by the smell of baked chicken, potatoes and corn commingling in the unpleasant way of a quickly cooling dinner. He stood in the living room clutching his backpack full of torn papers.

"Where have you been?" His aunt said, pushing away from the kitchen table. "You gave us such a fright!"

"The library."

"You fool kid," his uncle said, wiping his hands on a greasy napkin. "Get upstairs. Now."

Tommy obeyed, closing his bedroom door. He turned on the light in his room. It was a room that he slept in, but his aunt's sewing gear and boxes of unknown trinkets and clothes and Christmas decorations crowded one corner and half the closet. He was another stored object.

He felt heat rise in his face, in his fingers, like a pressure building from an unfamiliar place somewhere deep within him. It was like the feeling right before he cried, but this was different, bigger, and he knew tears wouldn't solve or relieve the pressure. He felt like his blood and viscera and very soul were growing too large to be contained by skin, and his head hurt so badly, and the weak light in his room grew brighter, so bright it blinded him, and when the bulb burst he turned away quickly, shielding his eyes from the shattered pieces.

When he looked again the light was still there, burning the same way as usual.

* * *

Tommy's aunt kept a box in her closet that was taped shut and had remained so all the time he had lived in this house. He had seen the box whenever she asked him to help fold the laundry scattered on her flowered bedspread, the cardboard muzzled on the top shelf.

One night, his aunt worked late at the store and his uncle was at the tavern watching the game. Tommy had been alone in the house plenty of times but had never dared to venture into his aunt's closet to take the box from the shelf. It seemed like sacred space. But now something had changed, like the particles in the air were different or someone had just pressed the keys to a locked door into his hand. He collected a pair of scissors and a roll of packing tape from the kitchen and dropped them on his aunt and uncle's bed.

Inside the closet, Tommy pulled the string to activate the light bulb. His aunt's shabby dresses and flowered blouses hung neatly pressed on plastic hangers. There was a small stepladder just inside the closet door. Tommy unfolded it, set it in place, climbed. He slid the cardboard box from its place on the top shelf. He shook the box lightly. He suspected it contained papers, considering the shushing sound and the weight. Now he descended the ladder and carried the box carefully to the bed. He stood over the box with the scissors, contemplating what he might find. Maybe it was just photographs and other mementos; maybe some legal documents he wouldn't understand. Maybe there was nothing of significance to find here. But he felt the time was right to slide the edge of the scissors through the old tape.

Tommy peeled the cardboard flaps away from the hidden contents. Inside were papers carrying words like *recommendation, hospital, commitment.* As he sifted, he found letters written in a frantic scrawl, his mother's handwriting. He unfolded one. His mother's words reached off the page and caressed his cheek, despite their agitated nature. *You can't leave me in here*, his mother wrote. *I can't protect him.*

The letter moved on to peeling paint, cryptic voices and treacherous nurses.

There was nothing more about Tommy.

Other letters were similar, punctuated with statements that left him chilled. *I am the only one who can save him.*

He felt sure there was a connection between her desperation and the nightmarish encounter. He should have kept his suspicions to himself, learning the hard way, ending up in Dr. Morgan's office with an all-too-familiar light in his eyes, now every evening forced to take a pill that made him feel foggy. It didn't matter what he said anymore; his aunt and uncle already thought he had lost his mind. What his aunt didn't know is that in the past weeks he'd been hiding the pills under his tongue and then flushing them down the green toilet upstairs.

"She was special," Tommy said later, when he'd re-taped the box and placed it back on the shelf. "That's why they took her."

His aunt dried her hands on her dishtowel and spoke carefully. "She might have been special. But she was also sick."

"That's what people say when they don't know what to believe."

* * *

On Saturday, they had a funeral for Tommy's mother.

"I won't go."

"We should all be there to pay our respects," his aunt said.

"But she isn't dead."

"We all need closure. It will get easier once we say goodbye."

"There wasn't a body," Tommy said. "How can you have a funeral without a body?"

"I know it's hard to understand. But there's enough evidence that she's gone."

"Not to me."

"Honey, she left a note. I showed it to you. Do you remember?"

He thought back to how reluctant his aunt had been to hand him the paper with his mother's handwriting. He read it, instead talking about the thing he'd seen in the field, the face he'd seen looking back at him. His uncle had left the house for the tavern, saying he couldn't occupy the same space as that crazy kid anymore.

I'm sorry, his mother's note read. *I can't be here anymore. Tell Tommy I'm in a better place.*

"Better place," Tommy had said, accepting the letter as evidence of her exodus from the planet.

"She means heaven," his aunt said. "She was hurting too much in her mind, and she just let go. It wasn't your fault. Some people just can't get better."

His aunt and uncle flanked Tommy as they walked up the church's front steps, their dark clothes encasing them like mothy wings. Tommy saw other townspeople and kids from his school who stood with their parents and avoided his eyes. Wordlessly, Tommy and his uncle followed his aunt to a pew, and they slid in next to an older couple. His aunt nodded politely.

In the sanctuary behind him somewhere, Tommy could hear a woman crying, and he turned, seeing Mae the Librarian. Other people's faces assaulted him with sadness.

The pastor's lamentations became a faraway droning. The church lights seemed to dim, and suddenly they went out altogether, throwing the church into darkness. A few of the women exclaimed and men twisted their heads around, looking for a culprit.

"It's just a fuse," the pastor said. "We'll take care of it. Shall we continue?"

After some time, when the pastor spoke about how Tommy's mother was a beacon to those who loved her, the lights suddenly came back on.

Afterward, before the potluck in the church basement, Tommy's aunt and uncle received a line of well-wishers who grasped their hands and offered platitudes with grave faces. Tommy wandered through the crowd to get outside in the fresh air, where he could be away from the oppressive smell of drugstore perfume, wood-polish and boiled ham.

Around the corner of the church, two men stood, backs turned, cigarettes in hand. They were talking about his mother.

"She went in the woods somewhere and offed herself," he heard the first man say. "Kid doesn't believe it. Come Thanksgiving, some poor dope with a deer tag will shit himself when he trips over her bones."

The other man guffawed. "And probably spill his beer."

They both laughed, then turned and saw Tommy staring.

"Oh, shit," the first one mumbled, and ground his cigarette under his Sunday shoe.

As he was walking away, the other man said, "Do you think he heard us?"

"Don't worry about it," the first man said. "He's crazy, just like her."

* * *

"I called and found you some more books at the Stevens Point branch," Mae the Librarian said, showing Tommy *The Hynek UFO Report* and *The UFO Experience*, both by J. Allen Hynek. "I'm afraid this one will give you nightmares; just look at that cover."

"I already have them," Tommy said. "Nightmares."

She sighed. "It must be so tough for you."

He thought she was talking about how difficult it was to find the answers inside the books.

On the way out of the library, something on the bulletin board caught his eye. A yellow flyer with black lettering and a drawing of a telescope read, Public Invited/Halley's Comet Viewing/University of Wisconsin Astronomy Club. He snatched the yellow paper and stuffed it into his backpack.

At home, he dropped the paper onto the kitchen table, where his aunt was peeling potatoes. "Can we go?"

She wiped her hands on a damp dishtowel and picked up the paper. She read it for a too-long time and finally said, "Madison's too far."

"It's not in Madison, see, it's at the state park. It's close."

"It's a school night."

"It starts at seven. It's done by nine, and we don't have to stay the whole time."

"Your uncle has his card game that night, so he'll have the car."

"We can drop him off, can't we?"

"We'll talk about it."

"I just want to see the comet."

"We'll see."

*　*　*

"The doctor said we should indulge the interest in space," his aunt was saying. "As long as he's getting his schoolwork done. They said he'll either lose interest eventually or it'll help him develop an—an *outlet* for his grief."

Tommy sat on the staircase, watching quietly through the railing. In the living room, Tommy's aunt hovered near the recliner, where his uncle sat, staring straight ahead at the television.

"It's a waste of time," his uncle said.

"It doesn't help to keep him away from it."

"That fool librarian isn't helping him any."

"They're just books. He's reading—what's the difference?" His aunt said. "Anyway, the school gave me the name of a therapist."

"I told you, it's not covered. We can't afford it. We should send him to his father. Let him take care of it."

"You know we can't do that. He's never been a part of Tommy's life."

"I didn't ask for this," Tommy's uncle mumbled, then turned up the volume on the Packers game.

His aunt stared at his uncle with a look on her face that Tommy had never seen, an expression with dark wishes swimming underneath. *Tomorrow, maybe you'll have a heart attack.*

Tommy quietly retreated to his room to sit in front of the bookcase that held his mother's books, to pull each one out one by one and touch her signature. After a while, Tommy heard his aunt ascend the staircase.

She appeared in his doorway. "All right," she said. "We'll go."

*　*　*

They stood with a cluster of other people on the ridge in a small clearing, silhouettes of pine and oak around them, the dark orange light fading in the west.

The astronomer, a slight woman about the same age as Tommy's mother, talked about comets, what they were made of, and how many passed by the Earth that were or weren't visible.

"Go on, you can ask her a question," his aunt said.

Tommy edged forward, raising his hand like he was in class. "Do you believe in life—on other planets?"

"Well, it certainly is a possibility," the astronomer said. "We don't have evidence yet, but we suspect there are thousands of worlds in our galaxy. It seems logical that we're not the only intelligent life out there, right?"

"Do you think they would come here?"

She shrugged. "Maybe they already have, and we just don't know. They may be far more advanced technologically than we are. They might not want us to know yet that they exist. It could even be that they've found a way to hide themselves here in order to learn about us."

"Do you think they've taken people away?"

Tommy's aunt stepped forward. "We should let her get people set up on the telescopes now."

"These are good questions," the astronomer said. "But we're getting into territory beyond my expertise. I suppose if I was from somewhere else and I was interested in Earth, like any good scientist, I might take some samples. That could include human life. Now, let's go and see the comet."

The astronomer moved on to a group of people clustered around one of the telescopes.

"You see?" Tommy said to his aunt. "It's possible."

"I never said it wasn't," she said. "But I just don't think it's what happened to your mother."

* * *

During the car ride home, after a long silence in the dark, his aunt asked, "Did you like the comet?"

"Yeah," Tommy said, and nodded absently. "Can I ask you something?"

"Anything."

"Am I crazy?"

"No," his aunt said. "I just think you want to believe your mother wouldn't leave you the way she did."

"But I know what I saw. I know you think it was just a dream, or my mind playing tricks."

"Well, I think when we want something badly enough, our mind can make it real."

"But at the church, what happened with the lights. Wasn't that her? Or *them*?"

His aunt gave him a sad look, the low dashboard lights illuminating her skin. "Honey, sometimes the lights just go out."

* * *

In the days after Tommy's mother disappeared from the hospital, he had waited for her to arrive, to collect him from his aunt and uncle's house to take him away. He was sure that was why she went missing from the hospital, to find him so they could be together again. He watched out the window for days, and when he failed to catch any sign of her willowy figure walking toward the house, or of any strange cars rolling up the long gravel driveway, he waited on the front porch. When that failed, he waited in the tree at the end of the driveway, his legs falling asleep as they hung over the edge of a thick branch, his aunt calling him inside when the light faded and dinner grew cold.

After Tommy waited diligently for weeks and his mother still failed to appear, he found the place by the river, near the clearing. He would stay there until he figured out what to do. He couldn't understand why his mother wouldn't come to him or what could have kept her from him. He couldn't fathom his mother not wanting him, yet he knew if she did, she would have found a way back to him.

He opened his eyes the next morning to find his aunt and a sheriff's deputy standing over him. His aunt was a gray bundle of anger, relief and tears. The sheriff's deputy said, "Come on, son, let's get you home," holding out a hand dotted with liver spots. Tommy didn't know how to articulate what had happened or begin to describe what he'd seen, so he simply stayed silent. But he had his answer. Now he knew there were things beyond his understanding, things that could tear a mother unwillingly from her son.

For a long time he wouldn't go near the field, instead retreating to the library, to absorb books, and to write questions and lists of clues in his black notebook, holding tightly to the possibility of their reunion.

* * *

From his room, Tommy heard the phone ring. Something in his aunt's voice carried up the stairway into his room. *Oh, lord. Oh dear.* He opened his door and quietly crept down the hallway, then stair by stair moved toward where he could see her through the railing on the green rotary, the coiled cord stretched taut.

"Are you sure?" His aunt said. "It was a match?"

His uncle pushed himself out of his chair and stood next to her.

"I understand," he heard his aunt say. "We will."

Whoever it was on the other end of the line must have disconnected, because his aunt handed the receiver to his uncle, who replaced it in the cradle. His aunt covered her face with her hands and sobbed. His uncle placed his hands on her shoulders and drew her close.

"We already knew," he said. "We already knew."

After some time, Tommy's aunt appeared in the doorway of his bedroom, holding a plate. She came over to the bed where Tommy was reading one of the library books, which he didn't bother to hide. She set the plate on the nightstand and sat next to him.

"Eat your cookie," his aunt said, "And then I have to tell you something."

"No," he said. "Not yet."

Tomorrow, everything will be different.

Once more, Tommy gathered his books and his spiral notebook, placed them inside his torn backpack and left his aunt. He navigated the stairway, passed through the living room where his uncle once again settled into his recliner, and retreated out the back door, heading for his quiet place by the river, under the massive tree in sight of the open field, where he could wait.

THE LAST DAY

He had said that thing I didn't want him to say. They had
planned for people to change their minds; there were others
who were willing to take my place. I loved him but not
enough. Now, though, standing here on this landscape
that took three years to see, I could only think that he
would have loved to see it. That last day I had wanted to
visit Cannon Beach. So we were there, in the heavy mist
and green morning, sea stacks partially hidden by hanging
fog, while his Labrador chased at foam and fragments of
driftwood. We watched the dog. I can't, I told him, and his
resignation thinly covered his resentment, but he held my
hand and we made footprints in the wet sand, and I thought,
this is all that's left of me here. My thoughts were a mix
of how I'd never hold his hand again or feel this ground
or breathe this air, and how much I was glad for it. After
the beach, we ate at an outdoor cafe overlooking the water,
wordlessly, and I fed pieces of chicken to the dog because
I couldn't eat. In a few hours I would get on a bus and be
taken to the facility where we would make our final prepa-
rations and that would be it. We weren't the first to go but
we would be the first colonists. We would be the ones to
make that place permanent, to establish the base for exploration, for mining, at least, and then to see if we could grow
more than scars. It was counterintuitive to believe we could
breathe anywhere else, but one by one we had unlocked the

mechanism that sealed our helmets. The air was just a little bit different, and we could both feel it and taste it, minutely heavier and sweeter, like orange blossoms after a storm. We could only describe things in terms of what we knew. With time, we would begin to build a new language. Though we had brought with us so little, we would always have our adaptability. We had learned to live with each other for three years in a tight space, and now that we had an entire planet it suddenly felt overwhelming and claustrophobic at the same time. We felt small. Some of us dropped to our knees, overcome by this thing we had accomplished or a knowing that this was really it, we weren't going home. Or maybe it was just relief, because really it had been a long and terrible trip. Our joy was tempered by the first task at hand, to scratch through the fine soil and bury the two who had died in transit, one to cancer, one to suicide. The procedure for disposal was supposed to be ejection, but we couldn't bear to do it, to leave them adrift, forever floating in a silent nothingness, unremembered.

A NIGHT-BLOOMING FLOWER

Someone turned my older sister into a bar of soap one night, and my father, bloodied and bruised, carried her into the house and handed her to me. A group of men growled and paced in the yard, as if expecting my father to toss my sister back to them. They pawed and tore at each other for a chance to rub her body all over theirs, to mix their juices with her foamy skin.

Gingerly I took her to the bathroom and laid her tiny squarish body on the edge of the sink while my father went outside to deal with the wolves in the yard.

"Hm," I said, trying not to upset her. "Hm."

"Is it bad?" She asked me from the porcelain. Someone had fashioned legs and arms for her, but one of her arms had been broken off. I imagined a man outside now spitting bitterness from his tongue.

"Well," I said.

"Don't turn on the water!" she screamed. "I'm too young to die."

"Don't worry," I said, and wondered how long it would be before someone turned me into something and what it might be, and if I would become so helpless and fragile and desired.

"Turn me back," she said.

"I can't," I said. "I don't know how."

I thought she'd start crying but she only sighed. "Just leave me alone for a second."

I closed the bathroom door and went to the living room window. I watched my dad fight off the group of men, mustering the last reserves of his youth, mixing that strength with his instinct to protect my sister. He swung a shovel at them a few times, and in the yard's motion lights I could see in his eyes that tonight he would win and tonight was all he could think about. He dropped the shovel and turned the hose on them, and finally they got into their cars and drove away. When they were gone, he turned and looked at me through the window, and his face looked so sad I wanted to run to him and cling to him, wished he could absorb me into him, let my blood become his again and let his heart beat for mine, or mine for his.

After a few minutes he walked toward the garage presumably to do things that dads do, and I went back to the bathroom where my sister had taken refuge, and knocked on the door.

She opened it. She was her normal self again, only maybe a little taller and thinner and prettier than I remembered her to be. Like a real girl.

She sighed again and looked at me.

"Don't ever grow up," she said.

"Okay," I said.

She closed the door and after a second I heard the sink running.

Mary stirred in her bed, her odd dream of the future dissipating. A train sailing above the clouds. Uniformed women with tight smiles that didn't reach their eyes. Had she been flying?

"Mary," Jack hissed, shaking her shoulder.

The room was black and for a second or two she forgot where she was. Every summer her mother and father sent her to stay with her Aunt Marion and Uncle Joseph and her two cousins, Jack and Alma. She always slept well in the big bed next to Alma, her body worn from a day of making bread, picking berries for canning, playing with the kittens in the barn and swinging on the big wooden swing that hung from the stately, canopied elm.

"Come on! We're going to go play Kick the Can!"

"But Aunt Marion will hear us!"

"No, she won't. We're going around the other side of the barn."

"Jacky, I don't know—"

"We've done this loads. Just be quiet."

In the darkness, Mary swung her legs over the side of the tall bed. Her heel accidentally connected with the chamber pot sitting underneath, and it clanged with a telltale volume.

The three children clung to each other, listening.

"It's kick the *can*, stupid, not kick the *shit pot*!" Jack whispered.

They giggled nervously and stifled themselves, grappling with their guts to hold in their giddiness.

"Come on!" Jack hissed, and grabbed Alma's hand. Alma took Mary's, and the train of children stole down the hall past Aunt Marion and Uncle Joseph's room. The door was open just enough for them to peep in as they crept by. Uncle Joseph snored obliviously but Aunt Marion was quiet and it was hard to tell if she was asleep or just pretending or what. Her aunt and uncle looked otherworldly in the moonlight, which threw long shadows across their skin.

The three children tiptoed carefully on the wooden floor, Jack and Alma leading Mary through the minefield of catalogued creaks and groans to the kitchen door, which Jack had oiled for just such an occasion.

He held it open and the girls plunged out into the night air like fireflies from an opened jar. For a time they forgot about the game and simply ran between the black pines, letting the cool grass hug their toes, their bodies feeling lighter in the forbidden territory of the night, as if weight were merely a consequence of being seen. They kept up their revelry until the sky started to change from charcoal to the color of Aunt Marion's hydrangea blooms, until the birds woke up and declared that life was once again under the dominion of daylight.

* * *

Ben Hart leaned over Jenny Fredrickson's shoulder, peering at the computer screen. Silently, he examined her story on the arrest of a prominent city figure on charges of sexually assaulting a 16-year-old girl.

"Well, here," he said, pointing at a phrase. "You can't say 'alleged rapist' because that could get us sued. You can say 'accused of raping.' And I'd move this graph up here so that it flows better. Other than that, it's beautiful."

"Gotta love our upstanding citizenry."

"No, shit."

The city editor, Marcia Kramer, yelled: "What's the E.T.A. on Wilson?"

"Coming!" Jenny yelled back.

"And we still need briefs," Marcia called back.

"Got it," Ben said, and checked the printer. Peter Gonzales and Melanie Marshall were lingering near it, and Peter handed him a short stack of papers from the tray.

"Remember the one from Clark County about the sasquatch?"

"Oh, right, the Clark County sasquatch," Ben said, flipping through the press releases.

"I still can't believe Kramer didn't make you go out there and do a story. That's the best thing that's ever happened out there."

"What do you mean? Other things happen?"

"Would've gotten Ray Krumbean on the six o'clock news." Peter said.

"I can't believe they sent that," Ben said. "It wasn't even April Fool's Day."

"Think about all the times Krumbean's had the sheriff's department out to his place to look at the strange lights floating over his backyard. And this they think is legit."

"That tells you a lot about the sheriff's department."

"You know, it was the prime opportunity for them to make him look like the dumbass that he is. Only Krumbean would've been too busy smiling for the cameras to notice."

"And trying to grab Marlena Albertson's ass," Ben said. "Has she been going to the gym or what?"

Jenny stood. "You only like her because she's good at reading my stories on the air," she said, and launched into an imitation of a movie Frankenstein. "Uhnnnnn! Teevee girl read good!"

"I can't believe he didn't call the camera crew himself," Ben said.

"So what was it?" Melanie asked. "I mean—was it a bear?"

"No, it was the worm at the bottom of Krumbean's tequila bottle," Peter said.

Ben flipped through the press releases, standing near a blue recycling bin.

"Three-car crash in Iron County, a motorcycle-versus-semi in Vilas, and an Alzheimer's gone missing in Lincoln. There. We got all we need."

Marcia's head poked up over a cubicle. "Call Lincoln County and see if they've got a mug of the Alzheimer's."

* * *

Mary grew into a lovely young woman, active in her high school and popular, walking through the halls with the confidence of a girl holding the knowledge that she was liked. Once in a while this confidence was bolstered by a happy secret—a clandestine love note, a smile from a favored boy, or the silky feel of her favorite slip under her skirt, the one that made her walk with an extra flounce in the hopes that the lace might show, just a little, since she'd worked on it so hard with her mother.

Allen Wallschlaeger wasn't her only beau but probably her favorite, she decided, even though Leonard Rickson's family had more money. Leonard's sisters were snobs, though, and she liked Allen's family as well as she liked Allen, except maybe for his mother, but she'd come around. She supposed sooner or later one of them would propose, and she hoped Allen would hurry up before Leonard got the idea and forced her to disappoint him.

One Sunday morning Allen came to Mary's house and asked her to walk with him in the light snow.

"Look," he told her. "I brought you a little present."

"For me?" Mary said, delighted. "You sly devil."

She snatched the package away and tugged at the string, which she flung aside without grace before tearing at the bronze, patterned paper. The gift was a small book with a red-checkered cover and the navy blue silhouette of two lovers—the woman impossibly thin-waisted and big-busted—kissing over a table. *Cooking For Two*, was the title.

"Oh, Allen," Mary flushed.

"Open the cover," he said. "I wrote in it."

She did. *To my sweetheart Mary, hoping we can cook up a great future. Love, Allen.*

Mary was to read that dedication many times after that, frowning over it, remembering that on that mild winter morning she hadn't noticed that under the dedication Allen also had written the date: *Dec. 7, 1941.* That day had propelled them headfirst into a dark future that got darker than Mary's youthful and naïve self ever could have divined.

*   *   *

We want more positive news, people said. We want more stories about education and health, they said. But Ben knew that people responded to readership surveys the same way they responded to questionnaires at the doctor's office about how many drinks per week they have: They say what they think the doctor wants to hear. They say what they think is the right answer, they say what will make them feel superior to the person reading their answers. But the reports from the online department proved they were liars: People wanted fire, sex and blood.

The story about the city official raping the girl undoubtedly would put the numbers through the roof and it would be followed closely by the brief on the fatal crash that Ben was working on now. Never mind Peter's enterprise on race and poverty in Marathon County, which he spent weeks researching. People wanted gore.

The Lincoln County desk sergeant's e-mail came through and Ben downloaded the picture labeled "missingmary.jpg."

* * *

Mary's cousin Jack was killed in the South Pacific.

Alma married a Navy flyer from Milwaukee who she met at a USO dance. He was a tall, skinny fellow who was nice enough except for the bad habit of sucking his teeth and laughing loudly at dumb jokes for the sake of looking happy even though his mind was still on burning planes that had plunged into the sea with his friends still inside. Only Alma knew his torment and never shared it, not even with Mary, not until after that old flyer of hers was grounded for good by a massive heart attack and a failed quadruple bypass.

Allen went to France, but he came home.

I don't know what's wrong with him, Mary often confided in Alma.

War changes men, sometimes, Alma would reply. *You don't know what he's seen or done.*

Why won't he tell me? Why does he take it out on me?

I don't know, honey. They just don't know any other way.

* * *

Ben played with the lede drowsily.

An 81-year-old resident of Northwoods Manor in Tomahawk wandered away from the facility and is suffering from Alzheimer's, according to the Lincoln County Sher-iff's Department.

He highlighted "and is suffering from Alzheimer's" and deleted it, then changed "resident of" to "Alzheimer's patient residing at."

He continued, thinking of the Packers game he was recording and wishing the guys in sports would turn down the TV so he couldn't hear the score.

Mary Wallschlaeger, 81, was last seen by Northwoods Manor staff when she was taken to her room on Wednesday night. Manor staff say Wallschlaeger was dressed only in a pink nightgown and that her slippers were missing from under her bed.

"Well," Ben mumbled, burrowing his chin into his hand. "Just put out an APB on the slippers, and then you've got your girl."

Sheriff's Department officials are urging area residents who may have seen Wallschlaeger to call the department or 1-800-ALZ-FIND.

Ben closed the document and sent it to the copy desk.

He knew, however, that before the brief was examined by early morning readers it would already be outdated and one of the reporters would be assigned to write an obituary first thing tomorrow.

He resolved to come in late.

* * *

Allen and Mary walked along in the snow. Mary struggled to keep up.

"Why did you change?" Mary demanded.

The young Allen stopped and looked at her, confused. "I don't understand."

"After the war. You were different. Something happened to you and you never told me what it was."

He seemed struck dumb, not as if he were surprised, but as though he had turned into porcelain.

"Why were you so bad to me and our girls?"

Young Allen didn't answer, but suddenly shattered into a thousand pieces and was blown away by a violent gale. The wind dissipated as quickly as it had arrived, leaving Mary staring at the moon and wondering why her knuckles hurt so badly.

* * *

Her face was nondescriptly elderly, thin and lined and unfriendly. Ben forwarded the jpg to the copy desk and sent the briefs to Marcia.

"Call me if you have any questions on the county board story," he said to her, pulling on his jacket.

She nodded without looking up.

* * *

"Alma, where did you go? Jack. Jack? Stop this, I'm scared…" Mary wiped a hand on her forehead, looking around her. "Isn't right, leaving an old woman alone like this. Not right. No manners. Oh."

A tree welcomed her and she dropped against the bark and slid to the ground, hiding her face in her hands, the blue-veined gnarled claws that belonged to Grandma Violet or Aunt Marion but not to her.

"Why did you do that to me? Why are you so cruel?"

The hands, the hands. Worked to the bone. Diapers, screaming babies, days of sickness and a mother-in-law that would have been better left somewhere by the side of the road. And the thing she hated the most: Cleaning his mother's rug with the carpet sweeper, which never worked.

Can't you get that damned thing clean? What's the matter with you? You don't do anything all day, why can't you do one goddamn simple thing I ask you to do – sitting on your fat ass, you goddamn lazy bitch. Clean it!

He had kicked over a wooden chair that day and Mary couldn't bring herself to look into his eyes because she was sure she'd see the devil.

She cleaned the rug, every last pill and fleck of fuzz, and five years later, after Allen's mother died, Mary calmly rolled up the rug, dragged it outside and set the fucking thing on fire.

* * *

On his way out of the newsroom, Ben caught a glimpse of Marlena Albertson on the TV news reading the press release about the Alzheimer's patient, showing Mary Wallschlaeger's picture and talking about how a search party had been organized by Northwoods Manor and the Sheriff's Department.

People would search for her, Ben knew. But they didn't know her and they weren't searching because they cared about her. They simply longed to be heroes in a world nearly devoid of them.

* * *

When Allen died, Mary had cried bitterly at the funeral, not because she missed him, but because everyone had stopped to tell her what a wonderful man he had been, how she must miss him so badly, what a loss it was indeed. No one knew her pain except Liz and Angela, and their sullen expressions weren't because of Allen, but because of her, because she hadn't left him, because she had allowed their pain to go on so long.

* * *

Ben had no idea why he turned the car north on Highway 51 instead of driving home that night, and he didn't tell anyone where he was going. He doubted he would find the search party—they would have already left Northwoods Manor.

* * *

Liz married an architect and moved to Seattle. They didn't have any kids. Angela got married to her college sweetheart, had two children, and divorced him ten years later. She lived in Texas and worked in an office. Her son won a basketball scholarship and was in his third year at Ball State. Her daughter was graduating high school and had aspirations of being a hairdresser.

The girls checked in with Northwoods Manor every week to make sure Mary was fine, or as fine as could be, and Liz managed to get back home every couple of months. Angela and the kids hadn't seen Mary in almost a year.

Or had it been? When had Mary last gone to see her children? Perhaps they were angry that she hadn't come. Perhaps they weren't her children at all, but her sister's. Did she have a sister? Why was it so cold in the summertime?

* * *

When he saw the flashlights in the stripped cornfield, Ben pulled the car over on the gravel shoulder and shut off the motor and headlights. Ben was chilled not so much by the November breeze but by the darkness and silence that was broken only by calls of "Mary!" that were dissipated by wind and distance.

He watched the flashlight beams scratch across the tilled dirt and scraps of yellow cornstalks, then opened his trunk to pull out a flashlight and a pair of boots.

* * *

Slowly, the sky changed from a soft pink to a delicate blue— sweet-scented and familiar like a shared secret, not unlike the summer snowballs of Aunt Marion's hydrangea bushes, the ones that Mary used to hide behind while Alma and Jack searched frantically, calling her name over and over again.

RESURFACE

Janine couldn't remember the color of the carpet at her mother's house, or when cigarettes hadn't clogged fat ashtrays balanced upon uneven piles of magazines or stacks of cardboard boxes. A fresh pack of Camels always within reach. So they figured it would be lung cancer. In the end it was breast.

"I guess you'll be happy to throw away everything," her mother had said, knocking over a shaky tower of round food containers. She bent to restack the plastic obelisk. Janine regarded the carpet of balled up fast food bags, piles of packaged rolls of toilet paper, plastic shopping bags from department stores, unworn clothes with discount tags. These were the most loved: The bigger the discount, the greater the treasure. Each year the labyrinth inside the house became more complex. Pillars of newspapers that contained potentially precious clippings, long-expired coupon fliers, yellowed mail. Brand new things mixed with trash and flies. The stacks had grown along with Janine and her brother, like a silent and better-loved third sibling. That offspring had grown obese and unkempt, massive and inert.

The frayed arms of the couch seemed to push back against the unstable mounds. Janine's mother had carved out a place for only herself, sculpting only a precariously narrow pathway to the bathroom. The kitchen was an inaccessible landfill.

"How did you let it get this bad?" Janine asked, the letter from the city crushed in her hand. She stood because there was nowhere to sit. "You can't stay here. It's not healthy."

Her mother stared into the rolling family room landscape. "You should talk. Look at you; there's nothing left of you." She stubbed out a Camel onto a ketchup-encrusted plate. "Doesn't matter, anyway. City gave me a month. Doctor gave me less."

Janine creased the letter into a tight square.

Her mother blazed another cigarette. "I'm leaving the house to you. Your brother will just sell it and stick the money up his arm."

"I don't want it." It would be better to burn the house and bulldoze the remains. The inheritance of baggage, the weight of resentment for each carefully saved item, each more worthless than the next, but somehow still worth more to her mother than Janine and her brother. "What can I do with it? It's not livable."

"It's yours, anyway. Your problem."

Janine squatted in front of her mother, tried to take her hand, for balance more than anything, but her mother resisted. Janine held onto the couch arm instead. "Mom. The hospice people won't come here. I need to take you to inpatient."

"No," her mother said. "They won't let me smoke."

* * *

When Janine was eight, her Aunt Maria signed her up for dance lessons.

"I can pick her up on the way," Maria told Janine's mother. "Sherie's in the same class."

"She doesn't need dance lessons."

Janine decided that day she would become a dancer. She ended up hating ballet, to her dismay, because she wanted to love something her mother hated. But as it turned out there were lots of kinds of dance, and Janine loved modern. Aunt Maria kept buying her lessons every year and Janine kept dancing despite her mother's protests. "We don't have money for that kind of stuff," her mother would say, carrying armloads of plastic bags into the house.

There was no place to practice at home, and even if there had been, Janine never felt like dancing while she was there, not even tight drills in her bedroom. The shadows were too long, the air too heavy. So Janine's English teacher let her dance in an empty classroom on days she stayed late grading papers. "I'll be down the hall," her teacher would say, and Janine would pop in earbuds and start shoving desks out of the way.

An arts school was out of the question. But Janine majored in dance at the state college and got a few gigs on cruise ships and one season in Vegas before shredding her ACL. It was terrible, this career-ending injury, but she'd had several years of salt air and lightness, of desert heat and the absence of whatever dark weight had pulled her mother down. Now, Janine was an office administrator for a chiropractor two states away and taught yoga to recovering patients, and once in a while she still taught dance part-time to middle-schoolers. Her mother liked to remind her of what she could have been. At least she had done something. At least she hadn't ended up like her brother.

* * *

Janine visited Roger in prison not long after their mother got sick. She remembered thinking how pointless it was for him to be there because he was high even then; the futility of the system, a pipeline to maintain his addiction. The dark circles under his eyes, the way his dirty fingers scratched at his forearms. She watched him until she realized he was staring at her collarbones.

When they talked, separated by plexiglass that necessitated the use of crusty phones, Roger took the news the same way Janine had—with a grim sort of resignation, not much else. He then spent a half an hour complaining about their mother. While Janine couldn't disagree with anything he'd said, she wanted to hear something more. Like what went wrong and why her mother had disintegrated year-by-year, why she had married a man that made her and Janine and Roger disintegrate along with her. Why they each tried to disappear in different ways. Why Janine had wanted to spend as much time out of the house as she could, even when Stan wasn't there.

"How old were we when Stan moved in?"

"Hell, I can't remember," Roger said. "What I do remember isn't right."

"What do you mean?" Janine asked, scooting the blue plastic chair forward. The leg caught on her white handbag, leaving a moon-shaped gray mark on the pleather.

"I remember Dad being there for my seventh birthday."

"But he left when I was a baby," Janine said.

"My point," Roger said. "I'm not remembering things right."

"Maybe he came back for the party."

"No. Mom said he was in California by then."

"Maybe it was Stan," Janine said.

"No, it wasn't Stan. When Mom had our parties, he went to the bar."

"My first memory is of him screaming at the TV and throwing something."

"My first memory is looking into your crib, except the way I remember it, there were two of you," Roger said. "And the dog."

"We never had a dog."

"Mm. Right."

"Maybe Mom was dog-sitting. Maybe she was baby-sitting."

"Who knows. I don't care."

"Maybe it was a dream," Janine said. "Maybe they all were dreams."

"My dreams are more real than my life," Roger had said, and then their time was up. He had a few years left to go, so he missed their mother's funeral, but Janine doubted he'd have come anyway.

The week her mother died, Janine had driven back and forth between her mother's house and a motel, sleeping fitfully for a few hours each night in the stale bed. One night she gave up and went for a run, feet stamping on wet ground until the sun rose.

"I put all of my hopes in you," Janine's mother had told her that morning, like an accusation. It was the last coherent thing her mother said. While her mother lay expiring, Janine had, as quietly as she could, started pushing armloads of things into garbage bags which she shoved into piles along the wall so the coroner could get her mother's body out the door when the time came.

* * *

Janine's mother died on a Friday and the dumpster was delivered the following Monday. Janine carried load after load out to it, lifting and dropping, filling the vast metal container with the remains of her mother's collected life. She started on the kitchen first, dragging a metal garbage can inside and lining it with a trash bag. It was easiest to use a snow shovel to scoop the trash into it. Used microwave containers, broken pottery, old bills that would never be paid, torn and used envelopes, used napkins and tissues, plastic grocery bags, empty containers of liquid soap, dried coffee grounds in used filters, jars of unopened but long-expired food, plastic cutlery wrapped and not, used and not. Foil pans with remnants of baked-on food, plastic and hard paper bowls that once contained a meal or sometimes still did. Before Janine had filled one bag, she'd seen several roaches and a mouse scattering from their disrupted cache. She pulled a facemask on and continued, then yanked off the mask and wretched in the still-dirty sink. On her elbows, she rested her head on her gloved hands, wondering if she should spend some of the little money she had saved to hire someone to finish this. She dismissed the idea, wanting it done, finding some sick relief in destroying the fortress built by her mother.

The experts on cable TV programs said hoarding was a way to fill an emotional empty space, to replace a loss. Janine could've told them that—and no doubt would have loved to air the blood and guts of her mother's childhood, to dangle her over the precipice of grief while the world watched and judged and said *Thank God that isn't me*. Wouldn't they have loved to unearth the relics that Janine's mother had buried under piles of bags and empty boxes that gaped with unused potential. Why she had married Stan the Abusive Prick. Why there had been no shortage of disaster. But what made one person navigate the pain and another to cover it with stacks of useless objects? What made you leave your children to fend for and protect themselves, but nurture and guard your pillars of years-old TV Guides?

Janine opened all the windows in the house, then lifted a pile of magazines that she'd stacked in the entryway and carried them outside. Her toes caught a rift in the disintegrating driveway and she stumbled enough to spray the armload of fifteen-year-old Redbooks across the rocky asphalt. She dropped to her knees, pebbles digging through her jeans. For some reason, her mind went to the time she first saw Stan hit her mother, how her child's mind had immediately wondered what her mother had done, how Janine imagined if she was always good enough that it would never happen to her. How the next time it happened, or almost happened, Stan had tripped on a throw rug. What Janine remembered, clearly incorrectly, is that the rug had been flat before Stan reached it and then had suddenly bunched, causing him to trip. Obviously, her child's mind had erased seeing his foot snag it.

Now, Janine heard footsteps coming from across the street, seeing a man stop next to the Dumpster. She released an armload of magazines into the container and ran a hand across her sweaty forehead, leaving grit behind. The man, who sported a ring of wispy gray hair and wore a tidy plaid shirt tucked into belted chinos, gazed at the yard, which was cluttered but no indication of what had been hidden in the house, hidden in their lives. The yard's accumulation included broken plastic chairs, ceramic plant pots with dead flowers, a single faded red Croc, lawn chairs with frayed seats; one that simply was an aluminum frame. Two plastic watering cans, one with a hole in the side. A desk with a pedal-operated sewing machine inside, a green wicker chair with a missing leg, TV tables, assorted coffee cups; some broken. Various plastic buckets and containers; some filled with dirt and attempted plants. An old bicycle, paint cans, appliances. Stacks of loose plywood.

"Thank God someone's doing something about this," the man said. "I've called the health department, I've called the police. I'd like to sell my house someday. You put so much work into a property and you can't control what happens across the street."

"My mother's dead," Janine said.

"Oh," the man said, his face looking flushed. "Oh, I'm sorry."

Janine turned to go back inside for another load.

"I didn't know that Betsy had passed. Wait. I just—can I fix you something to eat?"

"No."

He stared at her bare arms. "Well, it's hot—come inside and sit down and have a glass of water, at least. I'm Bill. I knew your mother, a little." He extended his hand.

Janine hesitated, then took his hand. "But you called the police on her?"

"Well, I—I hadn't talked with her for a long time. We used to talk, and then she seemed to want to keep to herself. Then," he waved at the objects in the overgrown yard. "Then, this."

"It was always bad. She just kept it out of the yard as long as she could hide it."

"Oh," Bill said. "I see."

Janine shaded her eyes so she could see Bill. "What did you talk about?"

*　*　*

Inside Bill's chilled house, Janine felt suddenly adrift in an expanse of naked space. A table with nearly nothing on it.

Clean floors with nothing to step over. She thought of a glacier, an ice floe.

"I'd have her over here for lunch, or tea, sometimes," Bill said, setting a cool glass of water in front of Janine. He sat at the round kitchen table with her, lowering himself carefully, settling his bones. His hands trembled a little. "I introduced myself when I noticed she had a faulty light over the garage. Thought it was a motion light but it kept coming on during the day when nothing was happening. I saw Betsy outside, when she still did her garden. So I went to tell her about the garage light. She used to talk about you kids all the time. You're the dancer, right?"

"When did you move here? I've never seen you."

"Must be twelve years now. My wife died. I think Betsy and I were both lonely—not that it ever came to anything, it wasn't like that, no. We would just talk."

"She never talked to us. Except to tell us how we had disappointed her."

"I don't think that's true," Bill said. "She would talk about you all the time, like she was bragging."

Janine scoffed.

"She did," Bill said. "But I read in the paper, about your brother's troubles. I asked Betsy about it, and I guess that was a mistake, because she stopped coming around."

The meth bust had been the big news in town for weeks. Roger had been addicted for a long time and turned to dealing to support his habit. Sometimes burglary. Once, armed robbery. In some ways, though, Janine thought he was smarter than her—he'd given up early on trying to win their mother's love.

"It was never enough," Janine said. "Anything we did."

"From what she said, that was all your stepfather. She blamed herself, for choosing that son-of-a-bitch. I think she felt responsible for Roger and his problems. The three of you kids meant everything to her."

"Two of us," Janine said, taking another sip of water. "There were two of us."

Bill frowned. "But your sister. What's her name—Stephanie?"

"Stephanie," Janine said, feeling the sound of the name vibrate inside her mouth. For some reason her mind went to the ice cream truck that used to jingle up the street, a thirty-year-old memory. "Where did you hear that name?"

"Your sister," he said again.

"No, I haven't got a sister."

"She talked about Stephanie all the time," Bill continued. "Talked about how she was a—a lawyer, had a nice apartment in the city. And children."

"You must be thinking of someone else."

"No," Bill said. "I'm sure I'm not."

"Then Mom must have invented her. A perfect child to brag about. Unbelievable."

"She couldn't have."

"She ever show you any pictures?"

Bill thought about it. "Well, I guess not."

"My mother had problems." Janine stood. "If you couldn't already tell by the yard and the house. She was always telling us about other people's children, clipping out newspaper stories about their wonderful achievements, sticking them on our fridge for us to see. She said if we'd been better kids, then Stan would have treated her better. It didn't matter what I did. I even got my name in the paper a few times, just to make her happy, but it wasn't enough. Roger got his name in the paper, too, didn't he? You saw it. 'How do you like me now, Ma?' he said. He laughed all the way to prison."

Bill's eyes focused on Janine's half-empty water glass.

"Sorry," Janine said. "Thanks. For the water, for telling me about Mom. It makes sense, it really does."

"I feel sorry for you."

* * *

After three days of steady work, Janine had the kitchen, the living room and the front entryway mostly cleared. It would take her another week to empty the house as long as she didn't stop to look at what she was throwing out, and that was easy when she was fueled by anger. She looked up, noticing that she'd left the hall light on. *I know I turned that off.*

She pushed the living room curtain aside when she heard the truck from the asphalt company. Today they would tear up the crumbling driveway and add the pieces of old concrete to the growing Dumpster mountain. Tomorrow, they would resurface the driveway. Next week, the carpet would be replaced and the painters would come.

Stephanie. Had she ever heard her mother say the name? It sat in the back of her throat, an ache of something gone and unreachable.

Janine stood at the entryway of her old room, the band posters still in place but virtually hidden by stacks of plastic tubs filled with God only knew. How many nights had she hidden here, headphones on, cranking up the volume to drive away the sounds of Stan and her mother screaming at each other, of things breaking, of her mother sobbing the next day over the lost objects but not the bruises. Janine bent to the floor, recognizing a frayed sleeve. She tugged on it, pulling one of her old sweatshirts out from under a bale of shopping bags. It was a faded, melon-colored sweatshirt with a hood, decorated with a crumbling rainbow print, a thing she wore to bed all the time to combat how cold her room felt all the time.

The phone rang, jangling her back to the present. It was a call from the prison and Janine accepted it.

"Roger," Janine said. "Hello?"

"Hey," he said. "What's going on?"

"The driveway guys just got here."

"Oh. How was Mom's funeral?" He asked like he was asking about a routine doctor's appointment.

"Fine," Janine said, lying.

"Okay. Did Maria and Sherie come?"

"Sherie did. A few of Mom's friends from way back—high school, I guess. They were there."

"Kinda bleak."

"I just had a weird conversation with the guy across the street."

"What'd he say?"

Janine told him.

"Well," Roger said. "You know where that came from, right? You had an imaginary friend named Stephanie."

"Did I?"

"Sure. You used to blame her for things you did. Knocking over a plant, slamming a door. *Stephanie did it, Stephanie did it.*"

The ache in Janine's gut grew into a sensation with limbs and consciousness.

"How old was I?"

"I don't know. Little."

"I don't remember," Janine said, but it was a half-truth. She wanted to ask him more: *What did she look like, what did she act like.* But it sounded crazy, to ask Roger to describe a person who never existed. Instead, they talked for a little while longer about the work being done on the house, and about a vocational class Roger managed to enroll in through a prison program.

"I'm clean," he said. "I'm getting better."

"That's good," Janine said, without feeling hopeful. The room seemed to fill with a familiar chill.

"It's going to be different now," Roger said. "You'll see."

"Good. I'm happy."

"Okay," he said, and Janine heard him take a breath. "I have to tell you something. I lied before. About the dog. We did have one."

"What? Really?"

Roger spoke in a rush as if he was afraid of losing momentum or fortitude. "Stan killed it. He did it in front of us. I didn't think you remembered, and I didn't want you to remember."

Janine's mind rifled through dark files.

"I don't mean to, you know, bring up bad shit or whatever. But I'm trying this new thing, where I don't lie anymore."

She absorbed this, the terrible thing that happened and how Roger's voice sounded different, like he was shedding a skin. "When did it happen?"

"You were probably three, four."

"I don't remember," Janine said, wondering what else she had pushed into the black hole of her memory. "How could—"

"I know."

Then Janine thought of the cat. "Jesus. What about Peaches? Mom said he ran away."

"I gave him to my friend Tim. Stan would've killed him, eventually."

"I don't know what to say."

If Janine had been old enough to remember the dog, would she also have numbed the pain of it with illegal substances? She had forgotten it, but she remembered the loss of some kind of innocence in the house. She remembered the onset of a darkness. Had she invented Stephanie as a way to console herself?

"Thank you, I guess."

"Yeah."

*　　*　　*

In Roger's old room, Janine found clear garbage bags full of new baby items. Stuffed in the closet, spilling out of it. Her mother had shown her, years ago. They had been purchased before Janine was born, the whites now yellowed, the tags with long outdated font and graphics.

"For when you get pregnant," her mother had said.

"I told you," Janine answered. "I'm not having children."

Lots of things were missing from her life, and she wanted it that way. She had relationships but never committed to one. Men liked that for a while and then got frustrated by what they couldn't keep for themselves. Janine longed for emptiness—an empty house, an empty body. She built monuments to nothingness.

She packed up the things that someone else could use, marking boxes for donation, and then threw away the rest. She dragged engorged cardboard boxes to the garage.

In Roger's room, at the bottom of a pile of candy wrappers and new boxes of feminine products, Janine unearthed a small untidy stack of random papers, including a child's drawing, pastel and crumpled. It was hers. She had drawn it for Roger; a family portrait with her mom at one end, round and gray, far from the children, separated by a house filled with scribbles. Scrawled below the figures were crayon labels: Mom. You. Me. Steffane. The 'me' and 'steffane' figures looked identical.

Who are you, Stephanie?

Vague images of playing in the driveway took a turn in Janine's mind. She was dancing with a friend, silly dancing, with a grainy hula-hoop and maybe roller skates. Laughing.

Janine went to Roger's window and pushed the curtain aside. The driveway guys had about half of the asphalt torn up. As a child, she had spent hours in that driveway, playing driveway games, drawing hopscotch squares, riding her pink bike in tighter and tighter circles, reining in a circus pony. *Ride faster. Faster.* Her invented friendship slowly re-emerged into existence, air bubbles rising from a deep lake.

* * *

She remembered the first day of school, kindergarten. Impatiently bouncing on new shoes, waiting for the bus with Roger, a third-grader, her sage, her source of wisdom.

Can Stephanie come?

No, Roger told her. *She has to stay home.*

Why?

I can't leave, Stephanie telepathed, twisting in a matching dress. *I'll be here when you get back.*

She'd had conversations with Stephanie like she was real. Roger was always off somewhere with his friends and Janine's mother was busy watching soap operas and smoking. Sometimes Stephanie waited for the school bus with her. She would invite Stephanie to come along on the bus, but she always wanted to stay in the driveway.

* * *

Later, when the driveway equipment outside rumbled to silence and the men began loading their equipment onto their flatbed trailer, Janine went outside.

"We'll start again early tomorrow," the contractor told her.

The concrete chunks of old driveway buried the junk in the Dumpster. The truck rolled away, and Janine regarded the uneven gravel and dirt that remained of her mother's driveway in the waning light, thinking of Stephanie, trying to picture her. But Janine could only imagine herself as a child, so she imagined Stephanie as looking like her.

"Are you still here?" Janine asked. The dirt absorbed her voice, soaked it into its dusty pores. She kicked at a clump of earth. In the back of her mind she felt something, not quite a memory but maybe a sensation of a memory, the ghost of one. The feeling of pressure, a shift in the air that transcended weak barriers like time and space.

Something glinted in the sunset. Janine bent, picked through the dirt. A marble. She remembered it; a blue cat's eye with air bubbles, a favorite. She had a sudden memory of Stan reaching down and grabbing her arm, kicking her pile of marbles, the glass rolling in every direction, Stephanie standing near, unflinching, of Stan slipping on the round glass. Janine squeezed the blue marble in her hand.

* * *

Janine sat in the now-empty living room on a folding camp chair she'd brought from her car, running her eyes over darkened carpet stains. She had a vague memory of lying on this carpet with Roger in front of the television, Stan and her mother on the couch, everyone silently mesmerized by the luminescence of the tube. She remembered a door slamming somewhere in the house, her mother letting out a yelp, Stan swearing and going to investigate. Janine remembered it happening more than once. A door would slam, a drawer would open. A light would flick on. One morning Janine woke up in the hallway, not sure how or why she got there, Roger shaking her awake and telling her to get back in her room before Stan found her. She remembered asking her mother why these strange things happened, always more frequently following a confrontation. *I don't know what you're talking about*, her mother would say. *It's just a drafty house.*

I want to live with Maria, Janine had told her. *I don't like it here.*

*   *   *

In Roger's old bedroom, Janine had set a few spare boxes of things she thought he might want. In one, she had packed family photo albums, stacking them vertically with the spines out. Roger could choose whether or not to keep them. Janine selected one, a cracking orange plastic thing with binder rings and yellowing magnetic pages. She opened it, seeing her mother's script inside the stained cover, listing the dates. The album was from when she was three years old. She put it back, taking out the one before, one she remembered paging through on a cluttered kitchen table.

But we need it for school, Janine remembers saying. *We're all supposed to bring a baby picture for the board.*

Just bring Roger's. They'll never know.

Why don't you have any baby pictures of me?

The album contained photos of her mother, pregnant and holding a diapered Roger, his sweaty dark hair pressed against her mother's chin. Her mother wore a dress patterned with large yellow flowers, sitting at the kitchen table where Janine remembered paging through the album, thinner than the others, missing some of its thick, plastic-covered pages. There were a few photos of Janine when she was almost two.

Just take one of those, her mother said.

*   *   *

Janine went back outside, carrying the box of albums. She set it down on the concrete step near the front door, peering out at the torn-up driveway.

Closer to the end of the driveway, near the road, something angular poked out of the gravel. Janine navigated the clods of dirt until she reached the pointy thing. She touched it with her shoe. It was a box top. No, a complete box.

She cupped her fingers and shoveled the dirt that mired it, grit lodging under her fingernails. A Gimbel's department store box, a once-gold cover with geometric shapes, a white base. A box big enough, perhaps for a hat, or a toaster. Janine scraped around the edges of it, unearthing a fossil. She couldn't prize the box from the dirt without tearing it, so she lifted the mangled cover and set that aside on the uneven driveway. The open box revealed a decaying pink towel bunched inside.

With both hands, she carefully lifted out the bundled pink towel. She found a damp corner and peeled back the ragged fabric, unrolling it. Whatever was inside was lightweight, delicate and hollow, like shells on a string. When she glimpsed what was inside the pink towel, she quickly set the bundle on the ground.

Bones. A skull detached from a body. Of a cat? *Not Peaches*. Her mother had kept other cats through the years, after Stan was gone, and thankfully had not hoarded animals, though it wouldn't have surprised Janine to have found animal bodies hidden here and there, maybe one secured under a tarp in the backyard, maybe one inside the drawer of an abandoned stove. But this was not a cat skeleton.

She continued peeling the towel away and looked closer. The head was too round, the hands and feet too familiar.

Janine sat down in the dirt. Looked around to see if Bill or the other neighbors were watching out their windows. She saw no curtains move, no round mouths. Buried in a Gimbel's department store box in her mother's driveway, a baby.

How had this happened? Could it have happened before her parents bought the house? No. Janine recognized the pink towel. This was her mother's towel. This was her mother's baby. Had Stan done it? Her mother? Her missing father?

The way I remember it, there were two of you.

"Oh, Mother."

This skeleton was well-formed, coherent. Had the baby been a girl? They'd be able to tell, if she called someone. Should she call someone?

Stephanie.

Janine gently examined the baby's skull. Fissures where plates joined, a place broken like an eggshell. How many cars had driven over this driveway, crushing the box? Despite its malformation, the cardboard had largely retained its shape, walls of earth carefully containing its secrets.

She gently placed the bones back on the pink towel, wrapped the remains, placed them back in the box. Janine sat with the remains until it was dark, glancing occasionally at the black windows of the house, where Stephanie had stayed, protecting her in the only way she could.

Tomorrow, they would cover the driveway.

FLOAT

There once was a woman who filled her apartment with water. But no one noticed, and she kept having to save everyone from drowning.

One day the landlord came by to collect her rent check, which was late, and while he was complaining about her tardiness, his lungs filled up with water. She grabbed him under the arms and swam up to the ceiling where she'd cut a trapdoor into the apartment upstairs. Somehow she managed to pull him up onto her neighbor's living room carpet and squeeze the water out of his lungs. Her neighbors sat on their couch, engrossed by a television program. When the landlord revived, he kept telling her that she must pay her rent on time, and if she was late again, he'd have to evict her.

Then there was the time the maintenance man came in to change the batteries in her smoke detector. She found him floating unconscious in the hallway, the hammers and screwdrivers flaring out around his belt like a hardware tutu. He spun gently in a kind of janitorial water ballet. She dragged him out the front door and dumped him on the concrete walkway. This time it took a neighbor's help to get him breathing again. When he coughed and sputtered to life, the maintenance man thanked her and said he had seen angels.

From then on she put up warning signs because she couldn't always be home to stop people from drowning.

But when her friends came to visit, they asked her what the signs were for, their questions popping out of their mouths inside wide bubbles. When they started to turn blue, she suggested they go outside and sit on the patio instead. As her friends talked, she noticed some of the water seeping out through the cracks around her windows. Her friends kept talking like nothing was happening, like her world wasn't pouring out onto the bricks around them. She asked them to leave. She caulked around the edges of the windows to ensure the water stayed in. People stopped coming by. Algae began to grow and fish arrived and the woman lived alone in her own ecosystem without interruption, as long as she kept the doors locked and the windows closed.

SPIRIT BOX

Kristin searched for a sound in the still air of the historic inn's guest room, holding up a hand for silence while Mark dropped the equipment on a rosy bedspread. Muted light filtered through warped glass, long shadows reaching over papered walls. Coming here at night would have been better. It was when the street noises dwindled, when quiet things felt empowered to become visible.

"Do you hear something?"

The voices were never voices, but more like the memory of sound—an echo off cavernous, sweating walls; a subaqueous whisper. It was more like a vibration. Maybe Kristin associated the not-voices with dampness because they felt damp, too heavy to rise from the place they once existed.

"Try the box," she said.

Mark switched it on, letting it cycle through radio frequencies.

Tch tch tch tch tch tch tch tch...

"Is anyone here today?" Kristin asked. "Can you say hello to us?"

They waited for the right radio frequency to be selected and used by an inhabiting spirit. The owners of the building, a historic inn, had called her, with the usual mix of skepticism and hopefulness in their questions. They'd purchased the inn several years ago knowing the stories associated with it—the apparitions of the anachronistically dressed, a light on or a door closed when it hadn't been, footsteps on the unoccupied third floor.

They believed it would add character, attracting adventurous ghost-experience seekers and giving a chuckle to the non-believers. It was like that for a while. Then it became more concrete and undeniable—screaming in the witching hour, a window slamming open, a cocktail glass hurled by an invisible assailant and shattering on the bar, cutting a guest; an oppressive feeling of wanting to be anywhere but there. What had started as spooky fun had turned nightmarish; the inn owners had to refund too many visits and pack up for guests who simply threw on coats and said to send their things later.

"Can you say hello?"

Tch tch tch tch telephone me tch tch tch tch...

"What?" Mark said. "Was that a 'hello'? 'Hello me?'"

"No, it said 'telephone me,'" Kristin said. "It's residual. An imprint."

"'Telephone.' When did we stop saying that, like a verb?"

"Did you ever say it?"

"Maybe my parents did. They had the kind with, you know. The dial."

"Rotary. I think the owners are wrong, then, it's not Marie. It's too recent."

Kristin had looked into the history of the Civil War-era building, which first belonged to Marie Marchand, after her husband died—under mysterious circumstances, of course. There were the standard old stories about poison and a wicked heart, of servants chained in the basement. Marchand had lost her fortunes to bad investments and the house went to the state, becoming a school for girls and then an asylum and then a guesthouse again. It was broken up into apartments in the 1950s, going vacant two decades later, brooding over a dying neighborhood until the young couple bought it with bad credit and misfortunate naivety.

"Give me the EMF," she said. Mark handed it to her.

Help.

That voice didn't register on the spirit box but inside Kristin's mind, part of whatever unexplained talent or gift or curse that had led her here.

On the electromagnetic field sensor, the green light flickered to yellow to orange and red. "Whoa," Mark said.

The meter went back to green.

"There are a lot of them."

"How can you tell?"

Tch tch tch tch tch tch tch tch…

It was another thing that was hard to explain. Individual voices didn't always surface; it was more a sense of layers and crumbling, a residual pastry. Kristin sensed whoever belonged to this 'telephone' voice wasn't causing the disturbances. The fathomless sadness and fear carried those words beyond linear time but did not carry physical force.

She handed the EMF back to Mark and twisted a small flashlight on, aiming the beam in the corners of the room where the light couldn't reach. Beyond the liability concern, the couple had been most unsettled by the screaming. They suspected it was Marie, the original owner, as one guest had seen an apparition in long skirts with a bustle.

Tch tch tch tch tch tch tch tch…

"What are we looking for?"

"Just looking," Kristin said.

Once, in an abandoned asylum, she found scratches on a floor—not words but hashmarks, marking time. Sometimes decades-old stains marked the wood, the telltale heart of atrocity. She checked for places where rickety fixtures could fall and for clues left behind by forgotten lives. The beam spotlighted only sections of decades-old wallpaper and cobwebs.

She set the flashlight illuminated on the windowsill and spoke to the room.

"Can you make this light go out?"

She glanced at the EMF reader in Mark's hand but already knew it would be quiet. Whatever she was waiting for was big enough that she would feel it first. She had known the feeling since her mother moved her to that house, her pubescent electricity mixing with the damp air of angry residue. Whether it was already in the house or she had brought it with her, she didn't know, but she quickly learned to recognize the change in air, the stale heaviness, heat that wasn't exactly heat. Sometimes an overripe smell, like musty fruit rubbed into upholstery. The innermost senses urging her to leave that place.

She couldn't stop looking for the source of that feeling. The wandering souls, the ones seeking retribution or closure, they sought her out, but they weren't the ones she was after.

The flashlight turned off.

"Whoa," Mark said.

"Okay, let's try again."

Mark set the EMF meter on a small doilied table, reaching for the spirit box. The otherworld was as complex as the physical one. Intellectually she understood the danger but instinctively she felt it now, signals jolting through the tree-like structure of her nervous system. She checked the EMF reader again but knew it was waiting. Like anything born of the dark, it despised the light.

The heavy air relented to cooler eddies of spirit, the others moving away. In this place, there was a hierarchy. Marie was here, certainly. She was only the beginning. The screamer was another, and the glass thrower, and the apparition. Kristin waited for the thing that held them there, the architect of pain.

The box pulsed, waiting to capture metallic voices through the filter of radio static. *Please.*

"I heard it!"

"Shh."

The stale air grew dense, the pressure growing inside her chest, like being held underwater. The air around her turned frigid. She held the spirit box into invisible space and asked for a name.

* * *

Weird things had started happening even before Kristin and her mother moved to the old part of the city. How many times had she felt the oppressive bubble followed by an imagined whisper? As a child she recalled her mother hastily packing their belongings in the space of an afternoon, moving them from their apartment across town, because of something Kristin had, for years, remembered as a dream. She'd been sleeping in her mother's room that night, for a storm or a nightmare, and woke to a scraping sound. She lifted her head, seeing her mother was already awake, staring at her dresser. The third drawer was open.

After a period of time that made Kristin believe her mother had fallen asleep, she finally stirred, moving toward the dresser in a way a person might move toward a nuisance animal. Her mother hastily pushed the drawer closed and turned her back on the dresser, smiling at Kristin in a reassuring way.

Then the drawer opened again.

The sound that Kristin's mother made still haunted her dreams, an unambiguous knowledge of horror. She remembered being scooped up and thundered from the room and out into the cold night air; amber streetlights illuminating their new reality. It hadn't been the first time strange things happened in the house, but it was the most blatant, the crossover moment when they couldn't ignore or shrug off or explain away something odd. When lights had gone on or turned off without warning; her mother would mutter something about surges and wiring. If a door slammed, a draft or uneven hinges. When Kristin woke up one morning, inexplicably sprawled in the hallway, tangled in her blanket, it was sleepwalking. Now, everything had changed.

They left that night only to have whatever it was follow or resurface in the new house, and from then it was a continuous sense of unease, like the wallpaper had eyes. Kristin felt herself changing, grappling with a presence or an ability she didn't understand. But mother had changed, too—smoking more, drinking, surrounded by a cloud of frenetic vibration, staying up late on the phone when Kristin thought she couldn't hear. *I think it was him,* she heard her mother saying one night into the receiver, the spiral cord stretching around the corner under her closed bedroom door. *Don't you think it could be? I told you about that night. No. I was afraid, what was I going to say? No, she doesn't know.*

There were things on the news back then, serious men with wide lapels and moustaches gravely recounting tales of missing women, unlocked windows and broken glass. There were pen-and-ink drawings of a dark-eyed man posted on telephone poles and in the window of a grocery store. Whenever they passed that grim face, her mother gripped

Kristin's hand in a way that made her feel like the delicate bones inside were about to crush.

"Why are you afraid of that man?" Her mother denied it once too often and finally Kristin demanded to know who he was.

"He's a bad person," her mother said. "That's all you need to know."

* * *

"Oh, my God, did you hear that?"

Over the years Kristin learned to sort her assistants into three buckets: The serious believers, the pot smokers, and the overexcited pleasers. They never stayed long, mostly because paranormal investigations didn't pay much but sometimes because something rattled them. They came to learn how to hunt ghosts for their own YouTube channels or for an odd-ball experience to add to their resumes; they never expected the feeling of ice-cold hands shoving them at the top of a dusty staircase or a demonic voice calling their names.

Tch tch tch tch Here tch tch tch tch...

"It said 'Here'!"

Similarly, Kristin categorized the voices. One, residual haunting, an impression of energy, something that wasn't really a ghost, but like a groove worn in time, a skip in temporal vinyl. Two, sentient—the ghost of someone who hadn't expected to die, or had something left to resolve. Three, something else. A spirit gone wrong, a poltergeist, power galvanized by fear. She was hearing a two and she was waiting for the three.

He's here.

"Who's here?" Kristin asked.

A long pause, frequencies scratching a pulse. *Killer.*

"What is his name?"

Static thumping.

George.

Kristin took a few seconds pause to control the bubble of emotion growing in her chest. "But he has another name, doesn't he?"

The scratching static. Mark's rising and falling chest. The guest room door creaked, moving open. "Are you here?"

Another voice, male and chilling.

Leave.

"I know what you did," Kristin said. Mark glanced in her direction. "We're not going anywhere."

I know you.

* * *

The man on the TV, the one on the faded fliers, went by the name George Winters. The Hacksaw Killer, the newscasters called him, because that's how he decapitated his victims, and the name was instantly catchy. Her mother operated on a hair trigger. She'd known him somehow; that much was clear to Kristin. She had processed what she'd heard her mother say on the phone and rendered the comments into a confession about her own origins.

To think this killer could be her unknown father both terrified and thrilled Kristin, and for this she felt a crushing sense of guilt. It drove an unceasing curiosity, a desire to be the one to catch him, to stop him. In her mind, she made herself the hero, the abandoned offspring coming back to slay the monster, the only one who could. She clipped out every story from the newspaper about Hacksaw, and when her mother caught on, she canceled the paper. It didn't stop Kristin. She waited for her neighbors to drop their old papers in the trash or stole them off their lawn. If there were no stories about him on a particular day, she'd refold the paper and put it back under the shrub where she found it. She pasted each article in a notebook dedicated solely to Hacksaw. Her obsession with the killer took seed not only because of her possible connection to him but even more, perhaps, because of the collective fear she felt surrounding her—from her mother, from the newscasters, from people in the neighborhood. It was the only time she thought other people understood how she felt every day. She began to believe it was his fault that she drew the inexplicable and unsettling activity, like maybe he'd passed along a part of his soul along with his DNA. It was all the more reason to find a way to end his dominion of fear.

* * *

After years of hearing the angry voices of lost souls, few responses rattled her.

The worst was in an old hotel, when it felt like something was pulling her essence through the floor, replacing her soul with ice, saying *now you're mine*. This, she guessed, might have been an elusive and rare number four, a thing that was never human. She'd felt the words in her head and the spirit box caught them, too. She felt herself wanting to surrender whatever had taken hold. Her then-assistant, a graduate student in psychology, had pulled her by both arms out into the parking lot, and it took Kristin a few days to lose the chill.

Now this.

You follow me.

"That's right," Kristin said, her heart thumping.

"What's happening?" Mark said.

"I know your name."

Say it.

"You say it!"

Hahahahaha.

* * *

She began to visit the crime scenes. Almost right away she felt a voice saying *Help me.* That was the first time the heavy stale-air feeling and the cold bubbles of chill had given her more; it solidified her suspicion of a deeper connection to this man. She used her birthday money to buy a spirit box to confirm what she heard. It was rarely as detailed as the words in her mind but it helped her to trust that it hadn't been her imagination, and later, when she began to bring friends along, it proved to them that she wasn't crazy.

"Who killed you?" she would ask, and she would sometimes hear *George* and sometimes other names and often nothing.

Kristin got arrested at age thirteen for breaking into the last crime scene with a friend, made to wait on a plastic chair at the police station while her mother signed papers.

"What were you thinking?" her mother asked.

It came out in a rush of accusation, a defensive attack.

"No," her mother had said. Her expression held such a twist of disbelief that Kristin knew her mother wasn't lying, that George Winters was not her father. Her mother explained that she'd had an encounter but nothing more, allowing him to drive her home one night after a party. "You were three or four years old. I think—maybe because so many people had seen him that night, it stopped him from—from what could have happened."

Kristin learned, finally, that her father was one of two other men, neither of whom would have been good for her or her mother, but they certainly weren't Hacksaw.

Was she disappointed? It was more like confusion, the inexplicability of her life.

The voices quieted for a while, like they were giving her space.

* * *

"I want to know where they are," Kristin said to the room.

Mark glanced at her. "Where what are?"

She had never stopped following George Winters. She was seventeen when a particularly vocal poltergeist led her to a shallow grave, and she finally found a sympathetic detective who had the time and resources to humor her. When his crews uncovered the mummified and headless corpse, he had asked her pointed questions, staring in that way people did when they were trying to file her into their own category. He sifted through "A" for accomplice and "I" for insane until he finally got to a letter he could live with.

He'd call her whenever they had run through every possibility on a missing person or had an antsy supervisor who wanted to clear out some cold cases. But the George Winters case continued to dog her, inextricably connected to her own conflicted feelings about what some called a gift. Why had she been cursed with the voices of the dead in her mind, or the terrifying ability to see specters walk across their own graves? Why had she been dogged by other people's nightmares in addition to her own, which only grew worse with every passing year? Growing up, her friends had noticed, seeing her pale when she passed by a cemetery or frown to concentrate on a voice that wasn't part of a crowd. One by one they fell away, distancing themselves from potential contagion. If she wasn't the blood and bone progeny of that freak of nature, how and why did she become this strange being, walking with one half of her mind in the living world and the other in a place that was no less real but terrifying to navigate? At least her imagined connection with Hacksaw offered some reasoning; without it, she had no explanation for why she was so different.

Kristin kept looking years after headless corpses stopped surfacing and the police assumed Hacksaw had died, investigating hauntings, tapping into the wake of psychic energy she felt whenever a body had not been put to rest properly. It was how she'd found the inn, years before the innkeeper called her, by accident or perhaps no accident, stopping her car outside, staring into the eyes of its broken windows. Foolishly, she had returned, ducking under the broken chain link fence with a flashlight and a recorder.

That first time, when she had broken in, there had been residual voices overlapping. She knew the inn was filled with death, but she had left without answers. Kristin sought out the last owners, searching records, looking for names. Twice she'd heard the first name, once on a midnight taping at a popular restaurant known to have been frequented by Hacksaw and once in a building that later revealed a headless body.

She suspected the inn held more secrets. She suspected it had been quiet because George Winters was still in charge.

And now she was back.

"I know you're here," Kristin said. "This is where you died."

"Who? Who died?" Mark asked.

Hacksaw.

"That's the woman again," Kristin said. "Is he gone?"

Go.

"Us? Where should we go?"

Basement.

"Come on," Mark said. "What's in the basement?"

"Will we find bodies?"

They waited for innumerable scratching beats.

Heads.

"Shit," Mark said.

Sudden cold, like a refrigerator door kicked open.

Bitch.

"This is what we came for," Kristin said, watching the EMF in Mark's hand spin up. "I want to talk to you, George."

Hacksaw stayed silent through the frequency shift.

Tch tch tch tch tch....

What would they find if they started digging in the basement? The police knew of eight and suspected more, twice as many.

"You have a chance to show the world who you really are. Come on," Kristin said. "How many are there?"

A silent pulsing of radio air.

"Are you afraid?"

Tch tch tch Are You? tch tch tch tch....

She recalled their pixelated faces stacked up in neat newspaper columns, how she sat at the kitchen table late at night, sleepless, and clipped carefully around the margins of their lost lives. If she could find them all, if she could put them all to rest, maybe she could offer not only closure to the families but also something like it to the young girl who stayed awake so many nights, trying not to see the death that lingered in the heavy space between flesh and the unknown.

"Yeah," Kristin said. "I have been for a long time."

The spirit box continued its staccato hiss, holding her in its mesmerizing, unchanging rhythm.

THE FLEDGLING

1

Gin
The Week of Malsol

In the sterile cave of the ambulance, Virginia ran a shaky finger over her locked phone screen and thumbed the call icon, tapping the most recently dialed number before remembering she wasn't supposed to call that number anymore.

But Rick picked up before she could erase her mistake.

"Gin, I told you I need some time," Rick's voice said.

She pulled the blanket closer to her body. The insulated walls that temporarily separated her from the scene outside seemed brittle and false, as if she could put her hand through them and be dragged out by the evil on the other side.

Fifty feet away, sixty feet away.

She held the phone to her ear. "Something's happened."

"What?"

She felt her hand cover her face. "I don't know," she said. "I can't—"

An hour earlier, all Gin had wanted in the world was an icy drink and for Rick to come to his senses.

She'd been trying to get home, stuck on the log-jammed Highway 41, backed up again because of—what? An overturned semi? An accident? Who knew. Her life felt like a series of accidents, mangled crashes for other people to stare at as their own lives traveled smoothly past her own.

She hadn't slept for more than a few hours since he had walked by her laptop and read a damning email from a coworker. Rick didn't exactly have the right to be righteous, but the deed was done. He had moved out on Tuesday. Or maybe he hadn't moved out, but he had left. She wasn't sure if he was coming back or if she wanted him to. But now it was Friday, and she still couldn't sleep. It seemed no one could, according to what people were saying on Facebook, but then her insomnia became a new thing, a living entity without antidote or remorse, like the baby growing inside her.

She had gotten in her car to see him, not thinking about it being Friday afternoon, about the weekend warriors rushing north. Then the traffic jam had rendered the line of cars to an unmoving caterpillar of metal and glass.

In the sweltering standstill, Gin had rooted through her purse for her phone. Should she call him again? He hadn't returned her calls today. He hadn't unfriended her on social media, though, so she thought at least maybe there was still hope. Maybe she was deluding herself. Her nerves felt uncovered, like layers of herself had flown away, along with the quiet heaviness of dream-laden nights.

She touched the Facebook icon and watched the page load, glancing at the windshield now and then to make sure traffic was still at a dead stop.

She swiped a finger through her homepage, scrolling through pictures of babies, food, a wedding, a teenage child's prom. Rick hadn't been online for the last few days, not that she saw, anyway. She didn't know what she expected. What would he say? *My girlfriend is a cheating whore. She likes getting e-fuck messages from her coworkers.*

She'd try calling again later. He'd come to his senses, wouldn't he? Gin flicked through the other posts. People complaining about air conditioning breaking down, being sick, insomnia, dealing with stupid people, cars that wouldn't start, more restlessness.

Third night without sleep, wrote her friend Michael. *Yes, I've tried melatonin, not eating weird food for dinner, stowing all electronic devices, and drinking #%&?*ing warm milk, thanks. I'm sure it's the heat. Thanks, global warming.*

Like.

From her friend Trina: *Almost slept but the neighbor's dog started barking at 3 a.m. Anyone know a canine hitman? Hit-pooch?*

Like.

Maybe it was a bad idea to Like anything. If Rick was online, he would see and think she was insensitive, ignoring the big fat gorilla of their breakup.

Gin gave up and dropped her phone in her giant purse, figuring it would slide to the bottom so that she'd require a mining crew to extract it again. She punched on the radio instead. Just in time for the NPR news summary, which offered her a listing of various horrible things going on in the world delivered in tones of prosaic gravitas. She tuned most of it out until they started talking about an odd story about strong solar storms, how people living in northern continents might view spectacular northern lights, but also might affect communications and radar.

My communication is affected, she thought, her mind on the stickiness of talking to Rick, but a growing sense that something more was, in fact, happening beyond her tumultuous feelings. She'd heard something about the storms a few days ago, too—had it been the evening news or something on cable? Invisible curtains of—what—solar particles? Space interference? Sunspots on top of the heat wave? Maybe the sunspots were messing with Rick's brain, making him see things that weren't there. Who was she kidding? He saw her exactly for what she was.

What I need now is a Big Ass Coke, she thought. The one you could swim in. Wouldn't that be nice? Swimming in a giant pool of icy Diet Coke. Please, now. They should have a resort somewhere that has a Coke pool. Somewhere cold. A resort in the Arctic, where those nice polar bears on the Coke ads live. Where we can see those northern lights they talked about on the radio. Where we can get a front row seat to the show.

Wasn't he being unreasonable? He was being unfair. He had ignored her, failed to understand what she needed, failed to talk to her. The rationalization stretched inside her mind like spiderwebs and held her will together.

Traffic rolled forward, inch-by-inch. Now she could see lights from emergency vehicles ahead, blocking both lanes. Dumb people were trying to enter the freeway from the on-ramp, and smarter people were refusing to let them on. Gin could see heat escaping from engines. There would be no getting through—more sirens came from behind and two cop cars made their way along the shoulder, parking horizontally in front of the three lanes. They were letting one thin line of cars get through on the shoulder.

Gin's gas tank was about ten miles from empty—she'd procrastinated filling up just in case prices came down—a massive hurricane along the Atlantic coast had jacked them up again. But she was as thirsty as her car, so it was time to suck it up and pay whatever the hell they wanted to charge for fuel.

She could just make out the exit sign ahead—it came before the crash site, and a lot of drivers were figuring out it was where they needed to go if they were going to get anywhere. Taking that exit would divert her a few miles out of her way.

"Screw it," Gin said. The ramp took her onto an overpass and diverted her away from the main thoroughfare. It was a couple of miles to the next off-ramp. A familiar sign launched out of the trees.

"*Yes*, Virginia, there is a Kwik Trip."

She steered into the convenience store lot and parked at one of twelve pumps. A man standing next to a battered green-and-white pickup tore off his receipt and gave Gin an assessing up-down look under the shade of his stained baseball cap. When she ignored him he opened the heavy door of his truck, hoisted himself inside and started the engine with a roar.

Despite the humid air pressing around her, Gin shivered as he drove away. She slid her credit card through the reader, tapped in the requested zip code, said 'no' to a car wash and 'yes' to a receipt, and began pumping. She leaned against her car, a single, hot breeze washing over her. Then the wind died and everything was stagnant again.

You don't talk to me, Gin, Rick had said. *Now I understand why.*

How dare he? He was the one who was closed off, silent and clueless. All of the ways he had failed her, just in the past week—she could stack them up like boxes and fill a room. She'd made a dinner for him and he hadn't told her he'd be working late; she planned a get-together with their friends and he said he already had plans. He left his dirty dishes on the countertop, expecting her to empty the dregs of his breakfast into the garbage, he'd failed to get the mail, neglected to pay the cable bill, which had languished on the coffee table for almost two weeks. She had won a new freelance contract at a health insurance company and he'd said 'uh-huh' like it was no big deal. So if someone else wanted to pay her a little attention, so be it.

The pump shut off abruptly, the sudden absence of sound startling her. Gin watched for the white tongue of her receipt, which did not appear.

Of course.

She aimed herself toward the store entrance. Despite the lines of diverted traffic passing on the road, hers was incongruously the only car parked at the pumps. Even the county road now seemed empty of traffic. She pushed the glass door, walking into a cold wall of air conditioning. The store also appeared abandoned—no clerk behind the counter, no harried customers. Gin scanned the perimeter of the store, brushing off an unsettled feeling, absently picking up items as if she didn't feel a growing sense that something was terribly off.

Twinkies. She tempered the unhealthiness with a bag of carrots and an apple. She canceled these out with a bag of potato chips. She walked past the refrigerated cases of pop and went right to the soda machine, selected the largest plastic cup, filled it with ice and sprayed it full of diet soda. She clawed the giant Diet Coke in one hand and the bags of food in the other, her wallet slipping under her arm. She dumped it all on the vacated counter.

She waited, looking for a bell to ding.

"Hello?" Gin called.

Nothing but the buzz of a flickering fluorescent above her head.

A panicky pressure ballooned in her chest, like she was suddenly the last person on earth, the lone survivor of a meteor strike. The last Kwik Trip, the last woman, the last Big Ass Coke.

She glanced out the front window just to see a pickup truck passing on the county highway.

Not alone.

Then she heard a noise.

A faraway sound, a wet sound. Like wet rags slapping on a cold floor.

Somewhere in the direction of the restrooms, beyond that, the Employees Only area. She left the bags of food but carried her wallet and the Diet Coke, which grew colder and heavier with each step.

"Hello, can I pay for this?"

A pair of running shoes connected to a pair of legs in blue jeans stuck out from underneath a curtain of dingy plastic strips that separated the public part of the store and the private—someone was lying on the floor, hurt. The running shoes twitched and shook with half-hearted kicks.

"Hey," Gin called, her heart pounding in her ears. "Are you all right?"

The white-gray hallway seemed to get narrower as she approached the twitching feet. That awful sound again, like water splashing, thumping, heavy fabric tearing. A metallic, meaty smell.

She pushed through the plastic strips. Another man straddled the person on the floor, his back to her, his convenience store bowling shirt covered in sweat. *He's trying to help him,* Gin thought. *He's giving him mouth-to-mouth.*

"Hey, do you need—"

The convenience store clerk reared back, startled.

She had stumbled onto a prank, or college kids making a film. Play acting. Fake. She couldn't be seeing what she was seeing. Gin's instinct shattered her rational mind. She felt her arms and legs turn icy. Loud sounds throbbed in her head. For that singular moment her mind shadowed out the clerk's face and she could only see the trembling victim on the floor—his jawbone, his bloody teeth, the muscle and blood exposed. Half a face.

Now she saw the clerk, and the rest of the world disappeared because he saw her, too. His eyes looked through her as if she were a plastic cup, empty and disposable. The clerk growled. Something was wrong with his face, too—a bloody darkness covered the place where his nose and mouth should have been. Was half his face gone too? He bared his teeth, which dripped strings of sinew.

Her legs were suddenly soaked—the soda had dropped to the floor and spun sugary liquid everywhere.

Gin tripped backwards through the plastic strips, which came alive and clung to her arms like tentacles. She felt her chest vibrate with the pressure of her screams and then suddenly she heard footsteps running from the front of the store, felt arms around her pulling her away from the hellish vision her mind had already tried to erase.

After that, everything spun in a torrent of hands grabbing, feet running. Men shouting, fists and bone, an ungodly howl, a woman screaming, fingers pinching her face. Cell phones and voices and pictures snapping. A hot, scratchy sidewalk and strange women hovering protectively, patting her awkwardly. Sirens and tiny, bright flashlights in her eyeballs. Men in blue shirts helping her into the back of an ambulance.

"*Virginia,*" she heard Rick's voice say, pulling her mind back to the moment, to the dead air between them.

Red and blue lights spun against the backs of her eyes, making her dizzy, blending with the vision of slippery blood on the grime-stained floor. Reality felt murky. She had no idea if she could articulate what she saw. She wrangled words for a living and now they had scattered like frightened sheep. Only the sacrificial lambs, the easy-to-catch, stayed near: Bad. Blood. Screams. Flesh.

And now Rick was waiting for an explanation, and she would fail him again.

"Never mind," she said, and wondered at the sound of her voice. It was coming from somewhere but seemed disconnected from herself. "I shouldn't have called."

"Gin," Rick said, "just wait a second."

The ambulance door clicked open, flooding the back with a wash of wet heat, a growling engine, the odor of diesel, realities destroying her tenuous illusion of safety. A man in a brown sheriff's uniform climbed in, and she could almost feel ghostly fingers reaching out for her through the open door until the officer decisively shut them out. He sat on the narrow bench across from her and flipped open the laptop he had been carrying under his arm.

"I have to go," Gin said, and ended the call. She stared at her phone, at Rick's number and his smiling face on the screen, and felt that he had suddenly become two-dimensional and would always be that way. The idea overwhelmed her with sadness.

The policeman introduced himself as Officer Jankowitz and asked her how she was feeling.

Gin shook her head. "I don't know how to answer that."

"Yeah," he said. "I wouldn't either."

He spent a minute tapping through a couple of screens and asked her to state her full name, address, birthdate.

"Virginia," he said. "I had an aunt named Virginia. Can you tell me what happened?"

He had a face like the man on the floor. Tanned skin, beard stubble. She looked away, resting a hand on her belly.

"I'll try."

2

Elena
Malsol + 25 Years

In the wide, empty room of the former retail shop, a half-dozen little virtual girls glowed like cherub-elves, approximating the movements of future prima ballerinas. Their stubby feet kept time to a classical piano tune, the walls lit with soft, undulating florals.

"Plié, and rise. Plié, and rise. First position," Elena said. "Anna, stand tall like a—building."

Like a giraffe. Like a tree.

"Plié and rise. Point and close. Show me first position. Right. Plié and rise. Second position. Plié and rise. Now third. Plié and rise."

"Change it to the spinny lights," a ghost girl said.

"Not the right music, Shane," Elena said. "Maybe next week."

None of them were older than eight, the youngest just four. They tested their feet and learned to dance but most would never see a stage, let alone travel outside a city. As a Malsol firstborn, Elena knew this herself. She had joined her classmates in virtual Cozumel, she had climbed a snowy Mt. Baker on a virtual trip with her mother. She had experienced the sensations of vacations, but each time she stood

101

in the center of her dark and empty store, she sensed the true expanse of what she didn't know.

The girl called Anna distorted and recovered, her signal arriving from the other side of the planet where lately the solar storms had hit particularly hard.

"Do my arms go here?" another girl asked.

Elena walked around to the back of the girl and moved her arms into place, touching without touching, her motions activating the girl's distant implanted neurosensor, which measured Elena's finger size and pressure and heat, translated to sensation on the girl's skin. The girl's arms moved along with Elena's motion. Elena's own sensor conveyed the feeling of the girl's baby flesh.

"They go here. Now, everybody, third position again. Good. Plié and rise, and rise. Fourth."

"I like this one the best," Anna said. "It's fancier."

"Front arm up a little more," Elena said to her. "Yes, that's right."

A chime sounded from the tab on the floor.

"End with fifth, and—hold," Elena said, and applauded. "Good. Okay, it's time to say goodbye. Same time next week. Be sure to practice what we worked on today."

They all said *Bye Miss Elena* and one by one, their little leotard-clad bodies flickered and disappeared as they logged off, the empty building seeming much darker without them. She had rented this space from her friend Spencer, who had claimed the abandoned strip mall after Malsol threw everything outside the city cube into the territory of fear. The store had wide windows that faced the darkness; these became her mirror wall. In the safety of night, Spencer had torn up the remaining rat-chewed carpet to create a wide dance space. Dead wires still dripped from the water-damaged ceiling.

Elena had pushed a small forest of naked mannequins to one corner and stacked their plastic bodies like tangled driftwood.

Elena's viewer flashed a message before her eyes. *Is class over? Will you come home?*

"Reply," Elena said. "Later, end." She sat in a dusty chair and removed her shoes, stuffing them in the bag. "Continue message: Do you need anything?"

I need you to come home.

"Messaging off."

Elena dimmed the makeshift stage lights and activated a neon aurora display on the wall behind her. She set her music, an ambient electronic thing her friend Aric had put together at his club in the center of the marketplace. It contained the elements she liked; interludes of quiet, cut by crescendo and bass. Now she danced for herself. As she moved her body, she cataloged each part in her mind; her toes, the ball of her foot, the muscles that allowed them to propel her body and stop at a groove on the floor. She felt the way her knees flexed, how her hamstrings carried the weight of her upper body, how her hips allowed her to twist and bend, how they moved on their own. How her arms butterflied or clawed. The tiniest muscles in her face, the breeze of movement fluttering hair in her eyes. It was easy to feel dead inside the tight space of the city. Beyond its solid walls there was a whole planet she could not see.

When she ended her dance, she stopped the music inside her head, collected the tab on the floor and wrapped it around her finger. There were permanent tabs all over the city, allowing the unreal to exist with the real.

She sat in the dusty plastic chair and replaced her shoes, pulled on her protective jacket, twisted her black hair in a bun, flipped her hood up and locked the store.

Outside, it was sol minus six hours. The dark beauty of the northern lights stretched from the horizon tonight, the visual aftereffects of solar storms sending charged particles into the ionosphere, now a shimmering dance of green and purple. The particles were not the danger, but Elena's mother insisted the night wasn't safe, and grudgingly Elena knew the covered protection of the city was safer. But after being shuttered inside all day with only unreality as a window, the short distance between the empty store and the enclosed city was worth the risk.

At night, cabin-fevered masses flooded the streets like a carnival. In daylight, people lurked inside restlessly. The terrified never left their dwellings. Elena's mother was among the people who lived mainly in the world that had been generated to replace the real one, common among those who had known and remembered what the daylight world had been like. Elena knew the stories. Her mother had said little about the life before, even though Elena had, since she could speak, begged her to share that world with her; Gin would only shrug and say *It was different.* That is, until Elena grew older and started spending more and more time with her friends on the market streets, daring each other with adrenaline games, like running out of the city through one gate and back in through the next. Then Gin wouldn't stop talking, not about the good life before, but about the things she'd seen when everything fell apart, things that still happened. *There are cannibals, do you understand?*

After Malsol, people who could afford to protect their residences put up walls or fences topped with razor wire or spikes, security gates, cameras, and alarm systems to keep them out. Then cities started to build walls. When they realized the sun was the biggest enemy, they changed the

way they built new structures, stacking commercial properties around apartments, condos and even residential homes,
onion-like, adding protective roofing, constructing cities so
residences were only accessible through tunnels of steel and
concrete. A window was a dangerous luxury, and if there was
one, it was made with a special smoked glass that blocked all
types of rays. All of this construction occurred at night, of
course, and continued constantly. Elena feared one day she
would be accidentally sealed in, boarded up and forgotten
in a city-sized coffin.

When she had rented the abandoned storefront outside
the city gates last year, her mother retreated almost completely into the virtual world, erecting figurative walls within
physical walls within walls within walls.

Now, Elena stepped out onto the wide, cracked macadam
that had been a parking lot. She stopped at the places where
silhouettes of corn grew from the cracks. She pulled the
tallest one toward her, tearing the husk away from the vegetable, shining the tab light from her finger. Nearly ready. She
could leave it another week and it would be almost perfect,
but she ran the risk of scavengers or a market seller taking
it. The only other tenant who had rented a nightspace—a
tractor parts dealer—had agreed to draw an invisible line
down the center of the lot, allowing Elena to take whatever
grew on her side if she left him whatever grew on his, and
he'd been good to his word. Still, Elena snapped the corn
from its stalk and stuck it in her shoulder bag.

Beyond the strip mall, in the light of the moon, nightfarmers worked fields in the distance, some on foot with
headlamps, others encased in massive equipment that rumbled along with a spotlight tracing the dark fields. Groups

of hired security people roved in huddled clumps with their shotguns.

Elena left the property, passing the fields, other abandoned and sporadically rented buildings, former warehouses and superstores, some of which provided dayshelter for the homeless. The monolith of the city loomed less than a mile away. *You don't know what can happen between here and there,* her mother had said.

The city's windowless outer buildings created a fortress around the rest, the buildings from before.

Elena glanced down a space between a massive building with a faded Sam's Club logo and another strip mall and saw something glowing. She saw no people. Had someone left a tab activated? The colors didn't seem right. The light moved but showed nothing, no image, no pictures, just a crumbled pile of light. Elena moved closer, curious about the malfunctioning light surrounded by night. She shone her own tab toward the unknown object, pushing her protective hood away from her face. She moved closer, hearing her shoes scrape on gravel and stone. When she arrived at the light source, she realized it was not a malfunction at all. Orange and red light danced inside waning embers. She lowered her hand toward the source of heat, drawing back quickly, feeling its intensity. The light shifted and changed where the heat rose, creating an invisible moving curtain. She reached for a stick to poke at the embers and watched the orange briefly intensify, then looked down at her hand that held the stick and realized it was not a stick at all but a bone. She dropped it on the cracked blacktop, where it landed with a hollow sound. Around the bone were other bones, flute-like rows of sawed ribcage, remnant sinew and congealed blood.

Skulls—human ones.

Elena stepped backward, slowly, the sound of her own blood pulsing through her ears. She turned and ran toward the safety of the city walls.

When she reached West Gate Nineteen, she scanned through, her heart pounding the way it had when she was a kid taking a dare. She threw herself into the anonymity of the familiar marketplace, slipping past a cacophony of trading stalls, hiding herself from no one and everyone. She wove past piles of scrap goods for sale, past stacks of remnant wood, past groups of children and women selling trinkets, past stacks of baked bread and buckets of candy, fabric collectors weaving rugs, cubby-hole stores filled with thrift clothing, electronics kiosks selling sensors and extra tabs, pharmacies, motorcycle mechanics, performers, and puppeteers. The scent of burning food induced an instinctive and painful nausea.

Down one alleyway lined with glowing storefronts, a group of young men gathered on crates watching a naked green alien woman glow-dance. Beyond them, a few people surrounded a gambling program, watching anthropomorphized holographic dice that fought each other. Two, then three remote players joined in, their avatars cheering along. Unreality intruding on reality. Inside her head, Elena quieted the street noise with more of her mixed music piped from her tab to her sensor. She headed for an archway that led to rabbit tunnels leading to the city center. A motorcycle snarled past her, and Elena pushed herself against the graffitied walls, pulling her bag against her body. She hadn't realized how rattled she was after seeing the things she saw outside the walls.

Ahead, avatar presences browsed the marketplace like electronic specters, glowing bluishly, including a tall man wearing a blazer who lingered in front of a stand of wilting fruit, testing the freshness of it with his non-fingers. "Hey, look at the sign," the shopkeeper complained, and the man glanced up at the chalkboard scrawl. *Look, don't touch. The fruit is fragile.*

"Sorry," the man's voice said, and then he noticed Elena and smiled.

Elena kept walking, moving past his digital presence, feeling his ghostly eyes follow her. She turned down a tight street where she knew one of the shopkeepers and encountered another small crowd, some of them children, blocking from view whatever was projecting from the tab. They bickered between themselves over whatever had captured their attention.

"Hey, you're blocking the road," Elena said. Two of the boys moved away and she saw they were not gathered around a projector tab, but a small, live bird, the reality of it creating a spectacle. The bird's feathers appeared damaged, malformed, and it attempted to fly but could not, and even if the circle of boys had not been blocking its way, it was likely that the bird was sunsick or possibly viralsick.

"Get away from that," Elena said. "You could catch the miteflu."

The boys and a couple lingering nearby moved away but a young man lingered as if protecting the sickly creature. His unkempt hair twisted in his face and his eyes carried the look of the wild and damaged, one of the chronically half-sunsick ill folk. The not-quite-dangerous, the not-quite-right. He bent toward the bird, attempting to corral it against the wall that lined the narrow roadway. His sodden shirt flapped open and revealed a trail of dark hair leading to the waistband of stained jeans. "Hi baby," he said to the ailing bird. "These beasts will go and you can be on your merry way and merrily to you."

"It's sick," Elena said. "You shouldn't touch it."

"You're ignorant," the man said. "Iggy Norant. Nor shall you be Ig, among the Ig."

"I just don't want you to get sick."

"You don't know me. I haven't been sick," he said, pulling at his matted hair.

"I didn't say—I'm going to call someone," Elena said, and directed her tab to notify the patrollers.

"*Don't* call, don't call. They are Ig. Norant. It can fly, just not today, you Iggy."

Elena shook her head. "Someone needs to take care of it. It's sick."

"*You're* sick, the whole *world* is sick, and you want every-thing to die, like your mind! I won't let them hurt it!"

Elena took a step back. "Sorry," she said.

"*Everybody's* sorry. Everybody's always sorry, and this bird will be sorry. You will be sorry."

"It's going to die. It's going to suffer."

"You don't know what suffering is," the crazy man said.

"Hey," said a voice behind Elena. She turned and a glow-ing virtual uniformed patroller stepped between her and the ill man. Elena explained the situation and pointed to the weak bird.

"You get out of here," the sunsick man said. "We don't need you. You're the problem, Not-Real man."

Another blue patroller appeared next to the first one, carrying a virtual electrobaton.

"Yup, it's sick," the first patroller said. He looked to the second patroller, who reached the baton out and sent a charge through the bird, electrocuting it. The ill man howled and dropped to his knees in front of the bird's carcass. The officer touched the virtual baton to the man and shocked him, and he fell, convulsing.

"Can't have you touching that thing," the officer said. "It's for your safety, sir."

When the ill man was immobilized, the patroller touched the baton again to the bird carcass, incinerating it.

"Won't be a problem now, ma'am. Thank you for your call," the first patroller said, from across whatever distance there was between them and reality. They stood around the unconscious ill man and waited, flickering, for their live counterparts, who presumably would drag him to the nearest suncase facility.

The boys who had initially gathered watched from a space against the wall, enthralled, not caring how the event ended as long as they were witnesses. The couple who had been standing nearby gave Elena a strange look and turned away down one of the marketplace's twisting alleyways, talking quietly. Elena glanced down at the spray of dark where the bird had once existed and suddenly, she wished she could back up time.

3

Gin
Malsol + 4 Months

The omnipresent sleeplessness had been the first sign that something was very, very wrong with the world, but like most first signs, it had been collectively dismissed.

So it was almost like an ethereal puppet master had decided to crank up the volume: Gin's encounter with the face-eating man had been one of many nearly simultaneous and unmistakable events that life was about to fall apart in a swift and terrible way. That evening, while Gin waited in the ambulance and tried to process what she'd seen, Officer Jankowitz had suggested the man had been strung out on bath salts. It made sense to Gin; she'd heard stories like that before. But then there were more reports of cannibalism, or of other homicidal and terrifying behavior, all things that people couldn't fathom or process at first because the incidents were so out of place and unexpected. These acts were fuel for salacious gossip when they involved strangers, but now people watched their elderly neighbor hack apart a delivery person or stood in horror as a friend's child captured and ate a small wild animal. It left witnesses traumatized, compounding the collective insomnia, and eventually they reacted by isolating or barricading inside their homes, boarding up windows and refusing entry to anyone, fearing attack, or contagion. They left unspoken the fear that they might already be afflicted and murder their own families. Later, everyone learned the widespread self-isolation likely saved lives because it kept people out of the sun.

At first, the prevailing theory was that a virus had impacted the brain, causing insomnia that drove people mad. When the sleeplessness was finally connected to unusually powerful solar radiation, people fled underground in streams, moving into their basements or boarding up windows. The authorities predictably acted too late, at first in denial, and later in disagreement on the best way to proceed or if there was even a way to proceed. Experts speculated that a combination of unusually powerful solar storms, shifting magnetic poles and thinning ozone had created greater susceptibility to dangerous ultraviolet radiation, particularly in people whose DNA or brain chemistry was already damaged.

The growing hysteria erupted in isolated tragedies that grew exponentially with the power of social media. Gin had opened the Facebook app later that night, debating whether to share what had happened to her, when her feed revealed a series of increasingly disturbing events recounted with a sense of incredulity.

Can you believe this? her friend Andrea said in a livestreamed video, in which Andrea shared footage from her window as a woman smashed her car windows with a baseball bat. *She lives on our street, I've seen her and we've waved hello on our morning jogs; I've never talked to her much less given her any reason to beat the shit out of my car.* Suddenly, the woman rushed toward the camera and viewers watched in horror as the crazed woman smashed Andrea's front window. The video stopped abruptly and people left stupid comments like, *Are you all right?* Gin had tried calling the police for Andrea, but no one answered.

There were so many others whose deaths occurred in real time, including Rick, who died just days after Gin encountered the face-eater, his posts rapidly growing agitated and nonsensical. *I'm going to Moab for the week*, he'd written. *Things are just too dramatic here.* A few hours later, a post that said, *People say there's a virus, maybe, but there's no reason for this ridiculous shit.* And then, *I know about the government hiding those experiments and you all are part of it.* People responded predictably: *What experiments?* and *What virus?* and *I'm not making up what I saw* and *It was awful, how dare you say it's not real* and *My family is traumatized.*

Gin had tried calling Rick again, thinking if he knew about the baby it might ground him, but the call wouldn't go through. Then another post: *I know what you're all trying to do to me and it's not going to work.* By the next day one of his friends posted that he had found Rick hanging in his basement. In a panic, Gin had packed her car that night with food and essentials, abandoning her apartment and driving herself to her family's cabin in the next state, a five-hour drive, arriving an hour before dawn. She'd said a silent prayer, grateful that she'd hung on to the cabin after her parents had passed away—grateful, in a sad and terrible way, that they were already gone and would not face whatever dangers were ahead.

Gin stood in the long weeds, rattling through her keys in the dark for the one that would open the cabin door. The cabin was simple, constructed with clapboard siding painted forest green, the windows trimmed in white, the paint flaking and crumbling. She ascended the simple cinderblock steps and turned the key in the deadbolt lock, the door creaking, and entered the dark cabin. The air inside was stale and ashy. She used the flashlight on her phone to get her bearings, shadows bouncing off dusty surfaces. The rustic cabin had no running water but was equipped with a simple hand pump in the kitchen sink. It had propane-powered appliances. On a shelf in the kitchen area, her parents had left oil lamps, a glass jar full of matchbooks, and a few bottles of replacement oil. Gin propped the phone on the kitchen table against the wall, working in the beam of light, taking one of the lamps and removing the glass chimney, adjusting the wick, lighting the lamp. She replaced the chimney and turned off her phone light as the warmer lamplight filled the cabin.

Gin carried the lamp, assessing. The cabin was heated by a woodstove in a central room, which contained the kitchen area and a living area with a couch, which was covered in taped, plastic sheeting. There was a screened-in back porch with a supply of wood for the stove. A couple of camp chairs were folded and propped in a corner. There were two small bedrooms off the main room, the mattresses also covered and taped, the bedding sealed in vacuum bags. Under one of the beds, zipped into a quilted fabric case, a shotgun.

In one of the closets—covered only by a sheet—her parents had installed shelving. On these shelves were stacks of toilet paper, shrink-wrapped canned goods and about a dozen dark brown pouches of what felt like vinyl. She examined one of these pouches.

MRE. Meal, ready to eat.

She hadn't taken her parents for doomsday preppers, but they had, in fact, spent quite a bit more time at the cabin during the last pandemic. Maybe they had wanted to leave her prepared for the next one. Everything stacked up, waiting for her, as if somehow, they knew. She touched the cylindrical cans that her mother or father had touched, and tears pooled in Gin's eyes.

In the closet of the other bedroom she found a collection of tools, several boxes of shotgun shells, two folded camp chairs, extension cords, a short ladder, two buckets, and a toilet seat.

The windows had already been boarded to weather long absences. Gin would leave the boards in place.

She wondered if she was safer leaving the car out front so any passersby would believe the cabin was occupied, or if it was better to hide it in the crumbling shed on the cabin property so no one would know she was inside, alone. She second-guessed herself and moved the car twice before leaving it in the shed.

She checked her phone constantly for messages from her friends, for emails, for social media activity, watching things deteriorate quickly, wondering how long the service would last as the insanity spread and deaths began to pile up. After a few days, she stopped looking. With a creeping sense of terror and despondency twisting into an inner storm, Gin considered ending her pregnancy, searching briefly for the nearest clinics, but only the emergency rooms remained open, and they were so overloaded with suncases that they would not deal with anything they considered nonessential. She collapsed, weeping, feeling simultaneously a sense of doom and deep relief. She wanted this child, despite everything.

She needed to protect herself—and the impending life inside her—from what was happening outside, but she also knew she needed to protect herself from what was happening inside her mind. She needed to talk to people. She needed to see that other people were surviving this. She wanted her parents. Gin went to the bedroom closet where they had stored the stash of food, assessing. It was enough for a few months, at the most. She reasoned that she needed to find fresh food for the growing baby.

Just before the turn onto the road to the cabin, maybe a mile and a half away, Gin had passed a mom-and-pop convenience store along the county highway. It was a place where tourists would stop for last-chance gas, overpriced groceries, fishing gear and vintage postcards.

One night, Gin eased the car out of the shed and drove to the end of the road, turned off the headlights, and watched the store for a while. She felt like she was casing the joint. It seemed to be operating normally, sometimes with a short line of cars—which were always packed full of items—waiting to fill up at one of the two gas pumps. She watched until the line disappeared, and she pulled the car up to a pump. Gin exited the vehicle, her heart pounding, and set the gas pump in place. It was an old-fashioned type with rotating prices. *Please pay inside*, a hand-written sign read. She filled the tank, trembling, her mind reliving what had happened at the convenience store at home, that horrific inauguration into the deterioration of society.

She filled the tank and eased the car into a parking place in front of the store, leaving her car between a pickup and a small SUV.

The store's windows had been sealed with large slabs of plywood. Another handwritten sign, written in marker on a neon yellow sheet of posterboard and duct-taped to the heavy wooden door, announced *New Hours: 10 p.m. to 3 a.m.*

Gin pushed the door open. Behind the front counter was an aging couple, standing in front of a wall of shelving that revealed a dwindling supply of cigarettes.

"Gas tonight?" the woman said, her voice jarring and strange to Gin's ears, as if she hadn't heard a human voice in years.

Gin nodded. "Some groceries, too."

"Sure, honey, take a basket."

Gin looked to where the woman was pointing and saw the stack behind her. She took one. "Thanks."

A younger man wearing an apron and rearranging some goods to fill an empty-looking shelf looked up and assessed her. He resembled the older man behind the counter and she guessed it must be their son. She flicked a nervous smile and he gave a nod in return. Gin felt her body coiling, ready for whatever unthinkable thing was waiting in the next aisle.

Instead, she found an older woman. This woman was about the age her mother would have been, with shaggy gray hair, shorter than Gin, wearing corduroys and a college sweatshirt, holding a shopping basket that contained a few cans. She smiled pleasantly at Gin, and just as Gin was about to move to the next aisle, the woman spoke.

"Wait—aren't you Virginia?" The woman said.

Gin stopped, puzzled—how could this woman know her? Then she remembered her parents telling her about neighbors on the lake.

"I'm Marie—I knew your mom and dad," she said. "My husband is John?"

Gin recalled the names. "Of course," she said.

"He's here, somewhere—probably looking at the fishing stuff," Marie said. "We were so sorry to hear of your parents' passing. It must have been hard losing them in the same year."

"Yes, it was," Gin agreed, not really wanting to talk about their consecutive illnesses. There had been too many losses lately.

Marie seemed to get it. "Well, I'm glad they kept the cabin—it seems a good place to have, what with everything."

Gin nodded. "I didn't know what else to do."

"Come on," Marie said, suddenly taking Gin's arm. "Say hello to John. He was such good friends with your dad; it will make him happy to see you."

* * *

As Gin's belly expanded, so did her relationships with her Marie and John. They sometimes visited each other in the witching hours, watching coverage of the chaos together on dim TV sets, or forgoing it for the night and playing a game of cards instead, and they taught her the games her parents had played.

Then one night Marie and John stopped in at her cabin.

"We're going to the cities," Marie said. "We think you should come with us."

John showed her a flier. *Safe housing available. Medical facility, food, amenities.* "We think it might be better," he said. "They don't know how long this will last. I don't know if Bill and Yvonne are going to keep the store open; they were planning to retire before all this happened, and they're not getting deliveries like they used to. Plus you've got a little one on the way and no hospital for miles."

"But the cabin," Gin said.

"You've already got it boarded up," John said. "Leave it. There's safety in numbers."

Gin stowed her car inside the crumbling shed on the cabin property, locking it with a rusted padlock that had no key. She packed the few things she had brought in her suitcase and gathered a few kitchen implements and towels into a grease-stained cardboard box. She filled a grocery bag with some of the MREs and a few other food items; she left the rest, believing she would return. Marie and John picked her up just after sunset and they wound their way down the county roads until they joined a stream of cars on the interstate headed toward the cities.

"There's so many people," Gin had said. "We'll be stuck on the highway when the sun rises."

"Probably," John said. Marie pointed Gin to the reflective sunshades she had folded up behind the seat.

"Will that be enough?"

"It will have to be. We have blankets, too."

Gin said a silent prayer and thanked the timing gods for letting it be November and not July, when they'd bake inside the car in minutes.

They were nearly in the city when the sun was about to rise, and John parked the car against the bumper of the SUV in front of them. Another car inched up behind them and parked the same way, instinctively gathering close, like ptarmigans huddling against arctic predators. They stepped outside to pee, Marie and Gin taking turns holding a blanket for each other, John not bothering, and in fact most people weren't bothering to hide themselves as they did the same, preparing for the long wait inside their vehicles. The three of them worked to block the glass against the deadly rays, passing a roll of duct tape between them. Gin dozed during the day, grateful for the back seat, occasionally waking when Marie or John would shift in their cramped space, and Gin's mind went to the times she had taken an overseas trip, trying to sleep in the narrow, upright spaces in coach. At least the days were growing shorter.

At one point during the daylight, Gin abruptly woke when something hit the car. It wasn't another vehicle, but more like a deer had run into the side panels, more unnerving because they couldn't see what it was. John and Marie woke at the same time, alert, and whatever it was ran into the driver's side again, and John shouted at whoever it was to *Get away*, and the sunsick person howled and ran into the car again, and Gin screamed, burying her head in her hands, fearing the windows would shatter, and John leaned on the horn for several seconds and the suncase yelled gibberish and clumped in heavy steps up the hood of the car to the roof, where he jumped up and down while John leaned on the horn. Finally, the man's footfalls sounded on the trunk and over the top of the car behind them.

John and Marie glanced over their shoulders at Gin, and they shared a look but said nothing, waiting in silence until their phones indicated the sun had set, and then John silently started the car again.

It was well into the night when they finally reached the place where volunteers in orange vests directed them to stop. A young man with close-cropped hair leaned next to John's window. "How many?"

"Three," John said.

The man took down their names and scanned their ID cards and then pulled a piece of paper from a pad. "Okay— you're going to pull ahead and leave the car where they tell you, and then you're going to head to this location. Only bring what you can carry."

John took the paper and the man moved on to the car behind them. "This can't be right," he said, and showed the paper to Marie, who frowned, then handed it back to Gin.

Anthropologie.

Gin looked out the passenger side window. "We're at the frigging Mall of America."

4

Elena
Malsol + 25 Years

Elena eventually reached the block where she lived with her mother in one of the innermost buildings, deep within the knotted network of streets, carrying a few food items from the market in her bag—rice and vegetables harvested by nightfarmers and the cob of corn she had taken from the parking lot of her studio outside the walls of the city. She shivered at the memory of glowing embers, of grizzled bone, of the incinerated bird. She didn't know if she would return to her dance studio and she didn't know what she would tell her mother if she decided not to. She could always ask Spencer if he had another place within the walls of the city but giving up the weekly escape would feel like turning in a key to an entire world.

Elena walked through a Southeast Asian restaurant, waving at the worker behind the counter, and then into a connected vehicle repair shop owned by a guy named Ronnie, who fixed motorcycles and scooters and lived on the ground floor of her apartment building. On the high ceiling in the repair shop, motorcycles in various states of disrepair hung lengthwise like sides of mechanical beef.

Ronnie saw her now and met her in the public pathway.

"She ask for anything?" Elena said.

"I brought her some food from Phoung's," Ronnie said.

"Thanks," she said, reaching for her bag to find some money.

Ronnie waved her off. "It was nothing. My grandma's like that, too, I get it."

She thanked him again and he lifted his wrench in salute. Elena continued through to the back of the shop and scanned her face on a reader. A gate in the back of the shop opened to the residence where she lived. Once inside, she turned the corner to the right and scanned herself into the apartment. Elena and her mother also lived on the ground floor of the complex, hidden from the sky by fourteen stories of metal, wood and concrete. Elena found her mother sitting on a soft chair in the main room.

"I've been trying to reach you," Gin said.

"I know, I had my messaging off for class. You got my response."

"I wish you wouldn't go to that place. You don't need to go there."

"I know," Elena said. "You've told me."

The apartment was like other apartments. It was plain, with plain eggshell walls. The kitchen was small and functional. There was an opening to a narrow hall with a tiny bathroom and two small bedrooms on either side. Both had eggshell walls. There were comfortable places to sit, and Gin had made these places her permanent home, the shape of her body permanently stamped in the cushions. Quiet ambient light radiated from ceiling tabs. Now, a tab on the table projected false windows on the plain walls, one of them showing a Pacific Northwest forest, the other, the Egyptian pyramids. If the windows looked the same, Gin would sometimes panic, forgetting that the view wasn't real, that the sunlight wasn't penetrating the apartment, threatening to turn its poisoned tendrils through Gin's and Elena's brains, turning them into flesh-eating beasts.

"I needed more of it," Gin said. "I wanted you to stop and get it."

Elena nodded. "I can have someone bring it."

"I could've done that myself," Gin said.

"Then why didn't you? You have plenty of fake friends to call."

"That's not fair. They're real to me. You know how many of my friends I lost at the beginning?"

"I know. I'm sorry. I shouldn't have said that."

"You don't know what it was like."

"I said I was sorry. I'll get it. Just let me get settled."

Elena moved to the back of the apartment to her small bedroom. She activated the tabs to the setting she liked; a Hawaiian beach at sunset, the tropical waves crashing rhythmically, a view that calmed her. She understood she hadn't experienced the things her mother had experienced, but sometimes she just couldn't stop herself from saying what ran through her mind. She felt her mother's judgment each time she left the apartment, and Elena knew she was just as judgmental toward her mother's decision to live her life inside. She dumped her sweaty and dusty dance clothes in the corner and selected new comfortable clothes out of a built-in drawer. She ran a brush through her hair and found her mask, then settled into her lounger to enter Refined Reality, now as one of the electronic specters.

Elena sighed deeply, attempting to relax her muscles. She situated the RRmask over her face—it fitted over her eyes, nose and temples, molded to her features, flexible and gelatinous. The RRmask communicated with her neurosensor.

She was back in the marketplace, having appeared in nearly the right spot.

The shop, a place that sold concoctions of herbal remedies and a few stronger things, was only a few steps away across the busy streetway. A scooter carrying a couple laden with bags sped by, one of the bags brushing Elena's virtual arm. At home in her lounger, Elena's arm shivered with goosebumps, feeling nearly indistinguishable from when the motorcycle had sped by her earlier in person.

She entered the store under the brick archway, smelling through her sensor the barrels of dried leaves, spices, seeds and grains, failing to resist the impulse to virtually sink her hand into a barrel. In her lounger, she felt the individual grains stick to her skin.

Other people, some physically present and some not, milled through the winding herb shop. Ahead of her, she saw the tall blazer-wearing man again, the one who had smiled at her in the marketplace before, the glow of his image flickering like a candle.

"I've seen you before," he said.

"Yeah?" Elena said, feeling less inclined to ignore him now that both of them were in a virtual state. "So?"

"So, I was hoping I could introduce myself."

"Why would I want to know you?"

He was older, perhaps her mother's age, with skin that crinkled in a not-unpleasant way around his eyes. His hair carried a peppering of gray. He wore a navy blue t-shirt under the corduroy blazer; the faded design appeared to be a flock of birds. He carried himself in a way that seemed to reflect a precarious balance of self-confidence and self-consciousness.

"Well, see, that's why I need a chance to show you."

"Well, I'm pretty busy."

"Me, too," he said. "My sister's not feeling well. I needed to find the compound."

That's what Elena's mother wanted. "That's too bad," she said, meaning to be dismissive, but it came out sounding genuine, and suddenly she felt like continuing the conversation. Sometimes it was easier with strangers. "Your sister is an indweller?"

"Like many of us these days."

"My mother indwells. All the 'real' experiences of life without actually having to live it."

"It sounds like you disapprove."

Elena sighed. "I do and I don't. I'm being too hard on her."

"It was tough, when it all happened. You're part of the NightGen. It's hard for younger people to understand."

The condescension gave Elena an instinct to pounce, but she realized he also sounded sincere. She was on edge because of what she'd seen on the way home, not wanting to admit how much it had frightened her.

"News is the storms are getting worse, at least on the southern side," he said.

"They are. A few of my students had a bad connection today."

"Students?"

"Dance. I teach kids."

"Oh, yes. Good. I'm a teacher, too. Well, professor. You know, I saw what happened," he said. "With the bird."

"Are you stalking me?"

"I can't help what happens in front of me."

"Yeah, that was a little crazy. That guy—he was a real suncase."

"No doubt," he said. "But, unfortunately, he was also right. The bird was just a fledgling. There was nothing wrong with it."

"You don't know that. It could have made a lot of people sick."

"Well, at the risk of sounding pompous, I do have a biology degree. Minor in ornithology."

"Oh, really. Get a lot of field study in, do you?"

"Well, no," he admitted. "That's a little hard these days. But the university has a great program regardless. And anyway, I remember from when I was a kid. Believe me, I can identify a sick bird, and that wasn't it."

She assessed him carefully, as well as she could while both in their virtual states. Now she saw his age in his dark eyes, the experience he carried from the daylight world. And something else behind them she couldn't pinpoint. He was tall, yes, and dressed in casual but tidy clothes, his skin exhibiting the tired cells of a sunless existence.

"If you saw, why didn't you step in?"

"The patrollers don't listen to anyone. Not academics like me. And anyway, the bird was doomed—someone else would have called if you hadn't."

Elena blinked. "Now I feel bad. I didn't know."

"Most people don't. You were trying to help."

They stared at each other's glowing forms.

"Why don't you have dinner with me?" he said.

"What? Where did that come from? I don't even know your name."

"Jack Larus. I go by my last name, usually."

"Dr. Larus. Sounds like an evil genius."

"Just Larus."

"I'm not sure that's better. I'm Elena."

"You see? Introductions are good."

"Well. I have to get back, my mother—she wants the compound, too."

"Sure," he said. "I understand. How about we talk again, just like we are now? Virtual, distant. If it's not real, we're not really on a date, right?"

"You're very persistent," Elena said.

"Tell you what; here's my contact. I leave fate in your hands, Elena," Larus said, and his image disappeared.

Watching the space where his image had been, Elena filed away his information, then followed a small group of real people toward the part of the store where she knew the compound was sold. She realized Larus had left without ordering it for his sister and wondered if he was simply giving Elena space, making a dramatic exit or had lied about needing it all along simply to have a reason to talk to her. She shook off the encounter and placed her order with the man who would send a delivery to the apartment. As soon as the order was placed, she blinked herself back to reality, gripping the lounge chair inside the quiet, empty, white cube of her room.

5

Gin
Malsol + 2 Years

Gin settled into the converted and mostly-emptied Anthropologie store with Marie and John and about sixty others, their narrow personal spaces divided by office-cubicle walls. They were the lucky ones; others who lived in other stores existed within imaginary boxes made of lines of tape. She languished on a rare mattress procured for the pregnant or sick, resting in the semi-privacy of her cube, reading books pilfered from the Barnes & Noble by the light of a left-behind Anthropologie lamp, on occasion agreeing to walk with Marie around the gleaming white pathways of the Mall of America, the massive skylights blacked over with sealant. They took this strange promenade past storefronts filled with traumatized people who had been forced to become families. On these walks, Gin accompanied Marie to the ladies' room, where they stood in lines to wash at the sink, just two people among the more than fifty thousand people that had been housed within the five hundred or so stores and offices and corridors.

The mall's entertainment sites continued operation, perhaps to distract people from their situation and help diffuse the tension. There were movies, roller coasters, mini-golf and other attractions. Parents with children frequented these places, the children happy with the ongoing predictability of the fun, the parents relieved that their children were distracted. Gin watched them with a hand on her belly, wondering what kind of world there would be available to her child.

Marie found a doctor who was living at the Alpaca Connection, and the doctor examined Gin, determining everything was as it should be, as far as she could tell without ultrasound and other equipment. The doctor and Marie made Gin an appointment at the hospital—at night—and the ultrasound confirmed what the Alpaca doctor had said. "Come back when you go into labor," the hospital doctor had said. "If it happens at night."

Babies rarely cooperate, so of course Gin's labor started at midday, so John and Marie helped Gin get to the ambulance when the sun set at about seven. It was spring, or getting to be, and the weather was rainy and cold. "We'll get you there," the emergency technician had told her, holding her hand. "There's time." All Gin could think about was the last time she'd been inside an ambulance and how much everything in the world had changed since then.

Elena arrived about midnight, so close, in fact, that the hospital staff debated whether she was born on the fifteenth or the sixteenth, and they finally settled on the fifteenth even though it meant her technical birthday was just seconds long. Gin held the baby in the crook of her arm, smelling the newness of her, watching the oldness of her eyes, wondering how in the world this tiny fragile creature would survive.

"Now what?" Gin had asked the nurse, who answered by talking about breast feeding, but Gin interrupted her. "No, I mean, now what happens to us? Where do we go?"

Gin had expected to bring the baby back to her cubicle next to Marie and John, but a social worker arrived an hour before Gin was to leave the hospital with Elena, and informed her that new mothers were eligible for placement in the newest housing systems in the city—safe places without windows, either converted office space or new housing constructed within the cocoon of commercial buildings. She went directly there, carrying Elena in a donated carrier. She sat on the floor rocking her because they had no other furniture. She wrote a letter to Marie and John—how do you address it, she wondered, and finally put their names, the Mall of America, Anthropologie store. She paid a kid in her new apartment building to take it there in the night, and expected he simply tossed the note in the gutter and took her money, but two nights later Marie and John came with her stuff, and theirs. They moved into the spare bedroom and stayed for the first two years of Elena's life, until more housing became available and they became eligible for their own place.

Gin would take Elena outside at night, the new normal for daily activities. Everything had shifted by twelve hours, with the "workday" now starting about nine p.m. Of course, she had no job—or not a steady one, at least. No need to produce website content when her client companies had closed. But sometimes the hospital system she wrote for still needed her to write press releases, most often about the importance of staying inside, or sometimes about new popup health clinics at unusual locations—a former auto parts store, a former fast-food chain. The hospital also partnered with aid organizations to deliver needed supplies to people. Sometimes Gin would volunteer for a few hours at one of these distributions, collecting a box of food or diapers at the end of the night and wheeling it back to the apartment on the top of Elena's stroller. Some of these boxes were marked with Chinese characters, and Gin wondered how these packages had traveled across the sea, where the light would come from all sides.

Elena was an active child and grew restless and irritable, so Gin took her out on walks enough to keep her occupied and calm, traversing the growing rabbit trails of human existence within the city walls. On nights when there was nothing for Gin to write, she would take Elena and follow fresh signs posted around the city that advertised locations of distributions, the items to be distributed often left a mystery until people were allowed to enter, one by one, the National Guard present to keep order in the cavernous spaces piled high with goods. There were excesses of certain things and shortages of others. Gin might wait in line for an hour or two with an irritated baby and discover they were giving away things she didn't need, like toaster ovens, or things she didn't have the skill or imagination to make useful, like bolts of fabric. Still, she took whatever they were giving, a growing pile of goods collecting in her living space. Sometimes she got lucky and was given a bag of toiletries or encountered a warehouse full of mountains of clothing to choose some items for her growing child. Gin wandered the piles in a bubble of anxiety, imagining where all these clothes had come from. Stacks of shoes reminded her of all the places people had walked and would no longer go. Gin began dosing herself on anti-anxiety medication to prepare for leaving the apartment, like so many others who were increasingly relying on the same. Eventually the government recognized the benefit in keeping people calm, developing "the compound" and distributing it widely and freely.

Eventually, Gin secured steady employment, a government job simply updating residential housing and population records from locally gathered information, sometimes stacks of handwritten papers. The nature of her work allowed her to see how many thousands of people had been displaced, had lost their lives, or were sunsick and unable to care for themselves. This gave her more reason not to leave the house. But once her income now allowed her to order the things she needed, which grew easier once the supply chain adjusted. Factories started running on shifts that coincided with the daylight, workers arriving before sunup and staying in the now-windowless buildings until after dark, deliveries going out after sunset. Overseas deliveries waned as shipping companies had more and more trouble finding crew who were willing to take the risk of traveling across the ocean. Things got simpler and plainer—no bright packaging, less variety. Days got simpler and plainer. Increasingly Gin relied on childcare to sustain Elena's desire for real human interaction, hiring teenagers to take her for walks or dropping her at a daycare within her apartment complex. Sometimes Marie and John offered to take Elena. Sometimes they would invite Gin to join them to get some cooked food at one of hundreds of entrepreneurial stands popping up around the city. "Bring something back for me," she'd say, and she'd catch Marie and John giving each other a look at her growing withdrawal from the outside world. Gin saw it happening, the long shadows of agoraphobia creeping in, but she wasn't alone, and the virtual world grew exponentially to accommodate a greater demand for an approximation of the old world. The compound had the effect of both muting anxiety and enhancing the virtual experience, making people feel more accepting of their new realities and more addicted to the unreality created for them.

She knew it.

She knew the reasons, and she didn't care.

6

Elena
Malsol + 25 Years

The night following the incident with the young bird, Elena heard her mother in her room talking to someone. She tapped on Gin's door. "Mom." When she didn't respond, Elena opened the door. Gin was stretched in her lounger, wearing her RRmask, shaking her head at someone only she could see.

"No, a different game. We played that last week and it was too complicated. No. Yes, let's try that one," Gin said, then laughed at something. "Don't be ridiculous; I don't win every time."

Elena closed the door, leaving her mother alone with her games.

It was sol minus forty-five minutes. She decided to go to the strip mall after all; she had a modern dance class for teen girls scheduled for later that night. Elena selected a set of dance clothes, including a wrap skirt, and suited up, grabbed her bag and pulled on a jacket. Her mother wouldn't notice her leaving. Her mother only noticed what was streamed from her RRmask.

When Elena exited the apartment building through Ronnie's motorcycle repair shop, she saw him talking to one of the mechanics. Ronnie excused himself and caught up with Elena.

"Hey," he said. "Benny's at the shop for tonight; I was going to head over to my friend Aric's club for a while— would you want to come?"

Elena stopped. "You know Aric?"

"Yeah, we were in the same class at school. You know him, too?"

"Sure, I met him at the club; he does the best mixes. I use them for my dance classes."

"Yeah, he's got a talent. So, how about it?"

He was asking her out. This was new.

"Um—well, I'm headed to my dance class. It starts in an hour or so."

"Oh, right. I could give you a ride." He pointed to a motorcycle.

She nodded. Ronnie handed her a helmet. She slipped it on, feeling encased in its heaviness.

"Looks good. Hop on."

She wrapped her arms around his waist. Ronnie pushed down on the kickstart and carefully drove along the public pathway through Phoung's restaurant and out onto the exterior street.

"Which exit?" Ronnie said loudly.

"Nineteen West," Elena responded.

He turned the motorcycle to the right. The ride was smoother than she expected, and not quite as scary, and Ronnie wove skillfully and smoothly through the maze of haphazard retail stands, piles of building materials, and delivery trucks; around chatting pedestrians, small crowds gathered around buskers, narrow pathway shortcuts through buildings, and winding rabbit trails through crowded, covered plazas. Even with the helmet on, she caught the odors of barbecued meat, wet garbage, burning fuel.

They passed a three-dimensional animated billboard featuring laughing people wearing RRmasks playing some kind of game in unreality. *PALpablexity*, the billboard broadcast through her helmet. *The fine art of fun and friendship.* Other billboards caught her ear, advertising a restaurant, a sports club, a gyroscopic skateboard. She reached up and turned her receiver off.

Ronnie turned the cycle to the west, zigzagging through the streets until he reached the Nineteenth, where he paused at the checkpoint, waiting for it to detect his sensor and open the gate. When they were through it and the heavy doors closed behind them, Elena tapped his shoulder and asked him to stop.

"Something wrong?" Ronnie asked.

"No. Yes." Elena told him what she'd found the night before, the fire and the bones.

"Maybe you want to do the class from home tonight," Ronnie suggested.

Elena thought about her mother talking to people who weren't there.

"No. I still want to go."

"I can stay with you," Ronnie offered.

"No, that's not necessary; the building is secure. But— maybe you could give me a ride home?"

"Sure," he said. "When should I come back?"

*   *   *

Elena's class had trouble connecting to the feed; the teens were all in Australia, New Zealand or Southeast Asia, and the solar storms had made communication spotty. Elena sent a message that she'd redo the lesson another time, disconnected, and instead ran through the routines for the next few classes. She had told Ronnie to come back in two hours. She could call him, but felt weird about it. She didn't know exactly what was happening between them. She could start walking and meet him at Aric's. She could wait. She decided on the latter, working through one of her own routines again for a while before stretching out on the floor near her bag.

Her mind jumped from Ronnie to the strange encounter in the marketplace with the unusual Larus, his blue form, his too-familiar, easy grin. She thought for a long minute—*what am I doing?*—then accessed his contact information. Instead of picking up a call, he appeared in her studio in his ghostly virtual form. Elena hadn't expected him to appear here, in her space, realizing now that she'd left her tab settings open for her holographic class.

"Well—the evil genius himself," she said.

"I saw your invitations were open—I hope I'm not intruding."

"I actually was planning to leave you a message."

"I can go, if you're busy."

"No. I mean—no, I'm not. It's fine. How are your birds?"

"Migrating. But the counts are down. Let's talk about something more pleasant. Does this mean you've decided on dinner?"

"No time tonight. Got a ride coming in a little while."

He nodded, and his glowing figure sat on the floor next to her. He crossed his legs. "But you called."

"Yes."

"Why?"

"I suppose you're—annoying, in an interesting sort of way."

He grinned. "Ah, well. Then don't get me started on the migration patterns of the black-throated blue warbler. You'll forget all about the 'interesting' part."

"Isn't it hard to be a birdwatcher if you can't be out during the day?"

"I can be out during the day. I can go out right from the safety of my home. And it's 'ornithologist.' Birdwatching is a hobby."

"Oh, well, pardon me. Ornithologist. And how do you keep track of what the birds do?"

"Well—I watch them."

"But can you really? There aren't any tabs in the remotest places. Don't you need to go where they are to really understand them? And isn't it a daylight sort of thing?"

"I study the urban migrations. How species adjust to these new dense population centers, which species are thriving, which are declining, or at least moving elsewhere. Besides, some species migrate at night."

"But not all—so what do you do? Watch from your couch?"

"Honestly, it makes my job even easier. If I want to know if a certain bird has completed its annual migration from Cuba, where it winters, I can just check for myself. I went there today, looking for a species, and found it, so I was able to get visual confirmation in real time that the migration, in fact, was still well underway."

"But it's not the same as really going there. I have students from the other side of the world, but they're still at home."

"It's still traveling," Larus said. "These are amazing times, Elena. You can go anywhere. See anything. It was hard for most people to do that in the real world. Travel was for people who had disposable income, and that was getting scarcer. And if you did have the means, you were busy with work and other things. Add terrorist attacks and pandemics, and you couldn't really go even if you wanted to."

"I suppose."

"How much time do you have?"

"A half hour?"

"I have an idea," Larus said. "Let's go to Thailand."

"What, now? I've never been there."

"Even better," he said. "May I?"

Elena nodded, and pulled her RRmask from her bag. He connected their ghosts, and there was a pause as he requested the right location.

Suddenly, Elena was standing next to Larus, their bluish ghost-forms positioned on Railay Beach on the hot sand in front of turquoise water and a limestone seastack covered with vegetation. Some of the other bluish figures nodded at them as they walked by or ignored them, just as they would in reality.

"Isn't it great? Look, there's a Bucerotida. A hornbill."

"This is weird."

"What, you've never taken a trip?"

"Yeah, sure, with my mother, virtually. Class trips. Things I did with my friends because they wanted to go and it was something to do. It was weird then, and it's weird now. It's beautiful, but it just doesn't feel right to me."

"I think participating in the world virtually is the best way to carry on a truly human existence, in all its splendor," Larus said. "People are so limited, otherwise, because without it, there's no ability to explore or connect with other places."

"Maybe, but if you live mostly in the unreal world, do you lose something in the real one?"

"I think calling it 'unreality' isn't accurate. This is really Railay Beach. It's a real place, and we're here."

"I just remember when I'd be on a class trip in school and not really appreciating what I was seeing, because 'unreal' is how it felt to me."

"But you're here. We're just experiencing it differently."

"We're receiving input and sensation that we're here, but we're not really here."

"Reality exists only in our minds. We're each living in different ones."

"To an extent."

"We still experience our lives and have the sensations of living, even if we never leave our apartments," Larus said.

"Like my mother. Or your sister."

"Or me."

"What, never?"

"I'm afraid, like so many others, that I've also succumbed to the secondary pandemic of agoraphobia. It's strong enough that I chose to live in a cloistered facility in Los Angeles."

Elena had assumed Larus lived nearby, in the Cities. "So we can never meet."

"We're meeting now."

Elena took a moment to absorb her feeling of disappointment, surprised by the impact of it. "What about your night migrations?"

"I can still observe them."

"When did it happen, for you? Indwelling?"

He shook his head. "A year, maybe two after Malsol. It was the same for lots of people. There were too many dangers, and, maybe, there was a sense that we didn't want to add to the horror by accidentally becoming the monster."

Elena's mind went to a time when she was in high school and she and her mother argued bitterly about Elena's desire to visit a friend she'd previously only met virtually. It would have required a trip in a train, which Elena argued was secure against sunlight, but Gin countered that it could never be truly secure. *It's not just about who or what is out there. It's what you could become if you're exposed too long.* In the end, her mother won, and Elena spent the weekend in her lounger, visiting her friend in ghost form. She recounted the event to Larus.

"I understand your mother, a little," Larus said.

"Maybe I understand her side a little more, now," Elena conceded. "But there's a loss of connection when we distance ourselves from the world."

"What is an experience, besides a collection of sensations, visual, tactile, auditory, and otherwise? You can smell the flowers on the air. You can feel the heat of the sun—without its dangers—you can feel the subtle roll of sand under our feet. You can recognize the expanse of the water and sense the danger of swimming out too far. How would it be different if you're physically present, if you have all the same sensations now?"

"It just is. We're humans, we know the difference. Over time we've removed ourselves from the natural world as if we're not part of it—most dramatically after Malsol. But we can't go on denying ourselves as organic creatures."

"Maybe the response to Malsol is the reason we're still alive. Maybe the ability of humans to adapt and integrate technology for survival is a part of our nature."

"To an extent. But then I think we become something else."

"Humans always become something else. Maybe that's what humanity is."

"I think our ability to adapt is part of our humanity, but it's only one part. If it had been up to me—I'm not sure I would have gotten the sensor implanted. I don't remember it happening, I was so young."

"Maybe you're right—maybe we've lost touch," Larus said, and faced the water. "Wow. Look at that view."

"It is stunning," Elena agreed. "I wish I could come here in person. I wish I knew what life was like before."

"It was different," Larus said. "I miss the sun."

"What else do you miss?"

"Human contact."

She looked up at his glowing face. "But not enough."

"Almost enough."

Elena heard the roar of a motorcycle outside the studio.

"I have to go," she said.

"Call whenever you like," he said, and his blue figure disappeared.

* * *

Ronnie asked Elena if she wanted to stop for a drink or something to eat on the way home, and, realizing she was starving, said yes. He turned off a busy street down an alley, then turned down another one, and finally stopped the bike in front of a storefront that Elena had never been to.

"Good burritos," he said.

He led her inside and she noticed the pathway from the restaurant led into a bicycle repair shop, almost a mirror of the entryway to her apartment building. She slid into a yellow booth and waited while he ordered at the counter. A mother and her two children emerged from the cluster of bicycles carrying string bags filled with vegetables. A group of teens walked through the Mexican restaurant into the bicycle shop and disappeared. Ronnie slid into the seat across from Elena.

"Where does this go?" She asked, pointing toward the entryway.

Ronnie looked over his shoulder. "This? It's more like a mall in there. There are lots of shops that way, and it opens into a public market. The apartments are above. Upstairs. You've never been here?"

"No, I think I've walked by but I've never come through here."

A girl brought a tray with two massive, foil-wrapped burritos and two drinks.

"Thanks," Ronnie said.

They unwrapped the food. Elena took a bite and sighed. "That is tasty."

"Right?"

They ate for a while. Then she said, "So—why do you fix motorcycles?"

Ronnie set his burrito down. "I don't. You saw the ones on my ceiling."

"But you fix other ones."

"Just something to do, I guess."

"But there's a reason you chose it."

His eyes focused on something in the distance. "I have this memory, from before. I was just a little kid, you know? But I remember riding on a bike with my dad. The sun on my face. The wind. I was too little for it, and not wearing a helmet—all the wrong things. I'm sure it only happened once. But it felt like—I don't know. *Joy*, I guess. It stuck with me."

Elena smiled at Ronnie's memory.

"And, now, I mean—people need them, right? Besides, we all need something to do. Like your dance school."

"Yeah. I guess so," she said. "Do you ever ride outside the city?"

He nodded. "Not for a while, except for today, to take you to your storefront."

"That doesn't really count. It's barely outside the gate."

"Oh, you mean adventure travel," he said. "Death-wish travel. Um, sure. When I was younger and more reckless. My friends and I took a few road trips. Timed it so we'd leave at sunset and arrive back at the gate just before dawn. We were crazy."

Something in his voice led Elena to believe it wasn't a happy memory. "When did you stop?"

He shook his head like he was gathering energy. "The last time we went out, like ten years ago now, there were three of us riding. My friend Marcus hit a patch of gravel, spun out, and his leg got all cut to shreds. He was okay, otherwise, but his bike was dead. We had nothing with us to take care of his leg, and he was bleeding pretty good. So we decided we'd better turn around, you know? He rode with me, so we had to leave the bike and find someone with a truck, later on, and hope the bike was still there when we came back for it. We'd barely gone a mile when this rabbit tears out in front of Angel's bike, and he missed it, but now he's skidding down the highway. You wouldn't believe it; it was like we were cursed. His ankle's broke, he's all cut up. Well, the three of us couldn't reasonably fit on my bike. There's no time to drop off Marcus in the city and come all the way back for Angel, and we're not going to leave any one of us to face the daylight. We had passed an abandoned gas station a few miles up. I take Marcus there, drop him, go back for Angel.

"Well, Angel's disappeared. He's just nowhere. I'm look-ing around in the place where I left him, and I know I'm in the right place because I had marked it on my sensor. Finally, I find this spot leading off the road where it looks like there's been a scuffle. Looks like feet dragging, and then I see blood. I'm calling Angel's name, knowing that I'm also calling attention to myself, but I stay on the bike, ready to go. I go off-road for a while, not knowing what I'm going to do if I run into him and—and whoever, you know? But I had to look. I looked for close to an hour, never found him. I knew I had to get back to the abandoned place where I left Marcus because the sun was coming up. So that's what I did. The windows had already been blacked out, and wherever they were broken, we covered with these old metal signs we found. We waited there all day, and I helped Marcus take care of his leg as best as we could. We called our friends. When the sun went down, before it was even really dark, our friends got there; I think there were three trucks, maybe ten people. We all went back to the site where we lost Angel. We picked up his bike and Marcus's, but Angel was just gone."

Elena watched him, stunned by his openness. "That's awful. I'm sorry."

"Yeah. It was a terrible awakening, I guess you'd call it. For years, I kept thinking about how we might have done it differently. We were never reckless about going out again. You'd think it would have stopped us completely, but I went out a lot after that. Looking, you know. I couldn't stop. I'll tell you something weird. I went out one night with one of my friends who had an off-roader. We ran into a group of people, I mean, almost literally. We thought we were dead, for sure. But they weren't suncases. They said they lived together in a small town not far from there and they showed us—they had rigged up the buildings on the main street so they were all connected, all the windows boarded up. They had torn up the street and planted gardens and put a fence around the whole thing. My buddy and I, we stayed with them for the day and they went out with us looking for Angel the next night. They knew of a couple of places where they'd discovered bones. I recognized Angel's jacket. We figured it was a group of suncases that got him. They must have heard us going by the first time, and after we turned around, they were there, waiting."

Elena just shook her head.

"I think it's safer now," he said. "I think there's fewer crazies. But yeah. I don't really go, unless there's a good reason."

She was grateful he didn't try to tell her she should find a different place inside the city walls to offer her dance class. She was grateful he thought taking her to her storefront was a good enough reason to leave the city gate. But the thing that happened to him, and the fact that she'd found fresh bones and a burning fire within a short distance of her storefront, was making her rethink the whole idea.

"My mom wishes I'd quit renting the store."

"What do you think you should do?"

"I don't know."

"It's dangerous," he agreed. "But here's the thing. I think those people were a little crazy to live out there like that, in their little town, but I get it, in a way. And I still love riding. I go around within the city, all the time. I know every street, probably. I love doing it. But I also feel—closed in. So when I gave you a ride to your store, it was just a short way out of the city, but I felt like it was the beginning of a journey, somehow. If that makes any sense," Ronnie said, then looked embarrassed and picked up his burrito again. "I just ramble sometimes."

"So you don't think I'm crazy, to want the freedom, even if it's dangerous?"

"No," he said. "I think you're human."

7

Elena
Malsol + 25 Years

When Ronnie dropped Elena off at the apartment, she found her mother in their small kitchen, eating cereal. Elena sat next to Gin and poured herself a bowl. "I heard you in your room, earlier. Were you playing games tonight?"

"Sure. I play most nights."

"With who?"

"No one," Gin said. "It was just a program."

"From that new company? I saw the advertisement."

"Yes. I'm just trying it out."

"Fake people?"

"What's the difference? Games are games."

"There are real people to play games with."

"Real people are complicated."

"What about the warnings? There's a health group says those virtual people are addictive—they make you want to stay inside even more."

"There have always been those warnings," Gin said, then gave an ironic laugh. "Besides, I never go out anyway. It's not like it will make a difference."

Elena didn't return her mother's smile. "I'm just worried. It would be nice to go out to the market with you. Ronnie showed me a great Mexican place; I could take you there."

"You can bring me some next time."

Elena finished quickly and rinsed her bowl in the sink.

"Did you have your class tonight?" Gin asked.

"I cancelled it. There are flares over Australia. Some of my class couldn't join."

Gin nodded and continued to eat alone.

* * *

In her quiet room, Elena found she had a difficult time sleeping as night turned into day and the sun edged its dangerous rays above the eastern horizon. She was safe, encased in an interior room of an interior apartment, but a tab created a tiny screen on one corner of the wall so she could see where the sunrise was. Even without the sunmonitor, most people had a sense of when things shifted, when things became deadly.

She tried reading. At about seven in the morning, she received a call from Larus.

"Let's go to the Grand Canyon," he said.

Elena reached for her RRmask. "Sure. Why not? Maybe a hike will help me to sleep."

Their blue ghosts suddenly appeared at the canyon's South Rim. Other ghosts walked past them on their way to the popular Mather Point, and some were returning from it. A precipice of red rock, brick and rust and terracotta and tan, plunged into an impossibly deep dive into the earth. Elena's sensor conveyed the wind at the canyon's edge, the scent of sagebrush on the air, and the idea of instability of being at the very edge. She felt a rush of adrenaline in her viscera.

"It's stunning," Elena said.

Larus took her virtual ghost hand. She didn't pull away.

"I miss the real world," Larus said. "But this is more real to me, because I can be here. And this is one of my favorites for birds. I can spot and enjoy hundreds of species of birds, whether it's a little scrub jay or a condor."

"Let's hike," Elena said.

"Sure," Larus said. "Let's do the South Kaibab Trail."

Their ghosts projected suddenly to the trailhead. Elena felt the gravel under her virtual hiking boots as they descended the rocky trail, overlooking sandstone and limestone cliffs, the hot, dusty air lifting vultures on its thermals.

"Wow," Elena said. "This is—wow."

"Like I said—one of my favorites. Don't trip on that," he said, taking her hand again.

"I feel like there's no bottom to this. Like if we fell, we'd fall forever."

"You might. Who knows?" Larus said. "The best part about this hike—we don't have to go back up at the end."

"That's cheating."

They hiked together for hours, finally going through a cool rock tunnel and ending on the footbridge over the Colorado River, surrounded by towering ancient cliffs.

"Still feel like you're not really here?" Larus asked.

"It's incredible," she admitted. "But let's say I'd been to the Grand Canyon in real life; I'd have more of a context for what we're seeing now. I'd feel more connection, more ownership of it."

"Do you need ownership to appreciate it?"

"No, that's not what I mean. Familiarity breeds connection, right? If we have an experience in which we make the journey to see a place, have the experience of being there, witnessing it, then it becomes part of us. If we see it again later, virtually or otherwise, it means something more. And that, in turn, builds a sense of responsibility for it. This, to me, is like watching a film. A good film, certainly, but I don't feel a sense of affinity for it the same way I'd feel for the actual place. I think we're losing that, collectively."

"But you grew up after Malsol. These are the only kinds of experiences you've had, so how do you know you'd feel differently?"

"That's not true, though. I've never been to Thailand or the Grand Canyon, and maybe I never will. Maybe I'll never do a lot of things. But I do spend time in the city, and at my studio, in-person. Feeling, touching, smelling—non-synthe-sized—are different experiences than having them virtually."

Larus kissed her, then, as they stood on the bridge over the green river.

"That's real," he said.

"This is still weird," Elena said.

"Relationships can work this way," Larus said.

"I know. I just need—to get my head around it."

"Tomorrow, then? If you enjoy hiking, I'll take you to Peru."

They disconnected, and Elena slept like she hadn't slept in months, a deep, lovely quiet, all-enveloping, complete and restoring sleep.

*   *   *

Hours later, Elena awoke to a sound that was out of place. She listened for a moment or two, trying to get her bear-ings. She was in her darkened room. The sounds came from upstairs, thumping—no, feet running on the ceiling.

Elena tapped a place on the wall and the clock appeared: 4:04.

Not found.

Through her bedroom door, she heard her mother say, "Oh, no."

Elena reached for the RRmask, a spike of fear running through her, thinking the unreality was down. She held the mask to her face and quickly accessed the last program, catching a glimpse of the Grand Canyon. The virtual space was fine. Elena set the mask on the quilt, feeling unsettled, fingers of sleep still clutching her.

More footsteps ran overhead. There was movement on her wall, a scrolling news alert: *Emergency in Central District, near Baily multiplex, shelter in place.*

Elena exited the comfort of her bed and opened her bedroom door, now hearing more voices coming from outside in the apartment hallway.

"What is it?" Elena asked her mother.

"I can't look," Gin said, trying to push Elena back into her bedroom. "Don't look."

Elena pushed past her mother, exiting the apartment, and entering the repair shop, which was empty. Ronnie was in Phoung's Restaurant, along with a few neighbors from the apartment building. They pressed against the street-facing windows, peering out the dark, protective sunshielded glass through cupped hands.

"What's going on?" Elena said.

"You should go back inside," Ronnie said, glancing at her but immediately going back to the glass.

She leaned against the protective windows next to Ronnie.

In the sun-exposed street, Elena saw a child, maybe about ten, sitting on the curb, talking to himself. "Oh, my God," she said. "He'll get sunsick."

"It's too late," Ronnie said.

The child suddenly released a snarl like a rabid dog.

"Somebody—call for help!"

"We've already called," Ronnie said, watching the child growling and foaming. The child stood and began tearing through a set of nearby garbage cans, searching for something to satisfy whatever hunger drove him.

"How could this happen? Where are his parents?"

"Could be an orphan. Maybe he's been on the street for a while."

"There are warning systems all over the city; he would have known to hide somewhere for the sunrise."

"He might already have been sick," Ronnie said. "The sick don't pay attention to the warnings."

"We have to let him in," Elena said.

"Are you crazy? He's too far gone."

The child flung a garbage can like it was a plastic drink container.

The spectators had anticipated seeing the arrival of glowing figures of virtual patrollers. Instead, live ones appeared from around the corner—two patrollers wearing head-to-toe yellow, space suit-like protective gear. They held electrobatons.

"They're going to kill him?"

"He's a child; they'll try to save him, but if he attacks—"

"This is horrible. They can't do this."

"They can. There was a lady in front of my old apartment, once, and they killed her right there. They say she cooked and ate her husband. Found his head in the stove."

"Stop. I can't hear this right now."

"Look, they're trying to help him."

The yellow-suited figures approached the child slowly, hands out, electrobatons dangling at their waists. They were speaking to the child, but through their masks and the thick glass, no one could hear what was being said. The sunsick child continued to root through a trash can, methodically removing bags and clawing them open, flinging aside cans when they failed to produce what he sought.

The patrollers grew closer and one of them pulled out an electrobaton, checked the setting, presumably ensuring it was on a stun level, and the other pulled out a set of wrist restraints. The boy noticed them now, growling at the patrollers. The patrollers positioned themselves in a defensive stance.

It appeared as if one of the patrollers was about to stun the boy. The yellow-clad figure lunged quickly, but missed. It enraged the boy. He leaped onto the patroller, knocking the person to the pavement, and tore at the patroller's protective head covering, managing to pull it clean off. The people inside Phoung's made horrified sounds, helpless to intervene. The unprotected patroller, who was a woman, tried to protect herself from the boy. The second patroller, who was slightly larger, shocked the boy with the electrobaton, attempting to stun him, but the boy's adrenaline was too strong in his veins, and he tore the electrobaton from the second patroller's grasp, now stunning the patroller, who fell to the pavement like stone. The female patroller, taking advantage of the boy's distraction, refitted her protective headgear and increased the setting on her baton, shocking the boy, but it only seemed to fuel his power, and he knocked the woman to the ground, then picked up one of the garbage cans and dropped it heavily onto her head. She was indisputably killed.

Elena screamed and Ronnie grabbed her into his arms, hiding her face.

She trembled violently. Another woman inside Phoung's sobbed.

"There's more. There's more patrollers now. Three, four of them," Ronnie narrated quietly into Elena's scalp. Suddenly, there were more shrieks from the crowd inside Phoung's. Elena gripped Ronnie as if she could wrap him around herself like a protective casing.

"They've—the boy is down," Ronnie said.

"Oh, god," Elena whispered. "Did that really just happen?"

"Yeah," Ronnie said. "Let me take you home."

* * *

Inside the apartment building, Ronnie handed Elena to Gin, who led Elena down the hall, into their private space. She led Elena back to her bedroom, helped her into her bed, arranging the blankets over Elena, remembering her as a small child. Gin sat on the bed next to her daughter's crumpled figure.

"I've seen some terrible things," Gin said. "I'm sorry you had to as well."

"I don't want to talk about it," Elena said, and turned her body toward the blank wall.

After a minute, Gin retreated and closed Elena's bedroom door.

Elena lay awake for the better part of an hour, the blank wall morphing into an endless, white fog.

Finally she reached under her pillow for her RRmask.

She called Larus.

"I saw something today," Elena said.

"I had a news alert. I understand it happened near you."

"Yes."

He nodded. "It's terrible. I've seen things like it. Many times."

Her blue ghost embraced his blue ghost.

8

Gin
Malsol + 25 Years, 3 Months

Gin understood there were particular moments for lots of people in the post-Malsol world in which there was a point of no return. It had happened to her, somewhat gradually, after Elena had been born, after they had lived in the comfort of the insulated and insular apartment for a number of months. But there almost always was a moment that the indwellers could reach to as the pivotal moment when they transitioned from being part of the real world to becoming part of the invented one.

For Gin, it had been a moment she hadn't witnessed.

John and Marie had stopped by to take Elena out for a stroll one night, saying they planned to go to the marketplace and buy things for a dinner with friends later that week. They invited Gin to come shopping with them and to the dinner party, both of which she politely declined. By that time, the invitations were perfunctory—they were used to her turning them down and Gin knew they'd express surprise if she had accepted. At that point, Gin stayed inside the apartment for months at a time, but she would still leave the safety of it on rare occasions—always for Elena. Once, an emergency in which Elena fell and hit her head, cutting it; another time, a special performance by a favorite children's TV celebrity in one of the mall buildings, to which Gin could find no one else to take Elena. But the night John and Marie took Elena to the market was when things transitioned from rarely to never.

They had come by early to collect Elena, maybe just after nine p.m., friendly as always, but now a step or two away from the close friendship they once had. They maintained the friendship now solely for Elena's well-being, which Gin recognized as a charitable act, knowing it was best for her daughter, though the price was a creeping resentment and sense of intrusion that Gin found increasingly more difficult to disguise.

They had exchanged pleasantries, and Gin had handed a bag of collected necessities to Marie, and settled Elena into the stroller, which John took and wheeled toward the door. Marie and John left with promises of returning at a certain hour, and when the apartment door shut behind them, Gin had a feeling of dread like none she'd ever experienced. She stepped out into the hallway to call after Marie and John, but they had already entered the exterior shop, which at the time was a kitchen appliance store. Gin had decided to let them go, not having any solid basis for what she was feeling.

About an hour and a half later, Marie called her from the hospital.

"Elena's fine, but John is in the ICU," Marie said. "I need you to come."

John had been stabbed multiple times by a sunsick man who had knifed seven other people and subsequently was killed by patrollers. Marie had been injured also, suffering defensive wounds to her hand and arms to block the slashing knife. Thankfully, she had shoved Elena's stroller out the way, tipping it in the process, and Elena's injuries were limited to scrapes, bruises and fright.

But the damage to Gin's already-fragile psyche was decisive, and with John succumbing to his wounds shortly after Gin arrived at the hospital, her brokenness scarred over. It was the last time she left the apartment.

The attacker had had no history of violence, no record of acting out in any sort of aggressive way. It had happened during a particularly strong set of solar storms, with multiple reports across the city of people suddenly snapping and losing hold of reality, and Gin knew it could happen to anyone—to her—at any moment.

After John's cremation, Marie boarded one of the protected trains and moved to another walled city. Gin, who by that time already had been taking the compound on a regular basis, now increased the dosage.

For the NightGen—those born after Malsol—very few slipped into the tendency to indwell, which some of Gin's generation called agoraphobia, others called common sense. The younger generation had grown up protected inside the increasingly complex layers of protective buildings and roofs. For the few that began to indwell, it usually occurred gradually, until something happened or the cumulative effect of daily worry of being touched by sunlight finally took its toll. For Elena, Gin knew immediately that what she had witnessed on the street could mean the end of her real life. For the past three months, Elena had proven her right.

Gin was self-aware enough to admit, however guiltily, that part of her hoped it would happen. It would keep Elena close and safe, for one, and her overwhelming sense of worry could diminish to a low hum in the background. It also would give Gin a permanent indwelled companion—the best kind, her own daughter. Maybe her desire had been thinly disguised and it was why Elena pushed back, why she rented that cursed storefront, fearing that one day she'd turn out like Gin.

If I don't do it, I'll never leave the apartment.

Why do you need to? There's room for your class right here.

And now, for the past few months since the sunsick boy had killed the patroller on the street in front of Phoung's, Gin had watched her daughter diminish into something she both recognized and didn't. The young woman occupying the other bedroom was her daughter but not her daughter, here but not here. Gin saw her even less than before as Elena remained ensconced inside her room, trekking around the world—something she had always wanted to do, except not in the way she had longed for, substituting her exploration with a virtual tour accompanied by Larus, ensconced in her lounger and enclosed within four white walls.

Elena cancelled her dance classes, too, and Gin saw the inactivity taking a physical toll, causing Elena to develop a small belly paunch, which Gin would see in the few moments when neither of them was under their RRmasks, when they both wandered into the kitchen. They kept their food stores replenished the way every other indweller did, with deliveries, including some from Ronnie, who sometimes stopped by unannounced.

"We could go to Phoung's," she heard Ronnie tell Elena once. "It's not even out on the street. Just through the shop."

But Elena now was as stubborn in her determination to stay inside the apartment as she once had been in her insistence to leave.

Gin knew how seductive the unreal world could be. She herself had a host of friends, some of them real (though like Elena's Larus, she'd never met them) and many of them unreal, invented by the various companies that provided programs for the indwellers. She had complex relationships with these friends, gossiped with them while they played games or shopped for groceries. Some of the invented ones were designed to be her age, with an imagined and very real background from the world before, so she felt like they understood her in a way that her newer friends never could. After all, they had been created by people who had lived it and knew what it was like. But she knew that made them extra addictive, because they appeared to share her lost experience.

Gin drew a terrible satisfaction from knowing Elena finally understood something about her now, this seduction of the unreal world. Yet it also carved a deep hole of pain that had yet to hit bottom.

"We went to La Digue Island, in the Seychelles," Elena told Gin one day. "The water was turquoise. The air tasted fresh and heavy, like after a tropical rain. There was white sand and granite boulders around us. We were out in the sun all day. I still feel it. My skin is sore to the touch, like I have a sunburn. Is that what it's called? Sunburn? Can you believe the sensor is that good?"

"Yes, to both," Gin said, and gave Elena a lotion that represented a sunburn salve. "You'll feel better if you use this."

"The water was so beautiful," Elena said. "And no one was around, so—well, never mind."

"Where does Larus live?" Gin asked.

"Los Angeles."

"It's just a shame I can't meet the person who spends so much time with you."

"We can meet in RR."

"Maybe sometime," Gin said. "You know, I remember you bringing home those National Geographic magazines from the library. You insisted you'd find a way to get to some of those faraway places one day."

"Well, now I have," Elena said, and retreated to her room.

Later Elena emerged again, only to ask if Gin had any compound.

So many times Elena brought home books about places on the other side of the earth that neither of them would ever see, and it broke Gin's heart to know it was never possible for her daughter to do anything that would take her outside of the city walls. She tried to introduce her to RRtrips as soon as she was old enough, and Elena seemed to enjoy them but no more than if Gin had read her a story or showed her a cartoon. And later, when Elena was older, it pained her when she started to complain that Gin never left the apartment like Elena's friends' parents, how other parents let their kids sign up for a trip across the city, or the train trip to see a friend for which Gin had vehemently refused.

And now, it seemed that as Elena experienced more of what the world had lost, she began to feel a greater connection to a life she never knew, paradoxically only finding it in the virtual space. When they shared a rare meal together, Elena talked about the places Larus had taken her—remote wildlife parks, bright and scenic beaches, the open ocean, bustling cities on the other side of the planet. And in Elena's voice, Gin heard something familiar: The false joy she felt at filling her days with a flurry of activity that in the end was simply hollow.

One night after dark, a few weeks later, there was a knock at Gin's bedroom door.

"Come in," Gin said, and Elena appeared in the doorway, looking peaked, a hand on her belly. "What's wrong?"

"Mom," Elena said. "I think I'm pregnant."

9

Elena
Malsol + 25 Years, 3 Months

"How is that even possible?" Gin asked her. "Ronnie?"

"No, I was never with him. Only with Larus."

"With Larus?" Gin blinked. "Well, then you can't be pregnant."

"We were intimate, though."

"Okay. But that was virtual."

"It seemed real," Elena said. "Like real in a non-RR sort of way. And I haven't had a period since I started seeing him, and look—" She displayed her rounded silhouette.

"You're just putting on a little weight," Gin said. "You haven't been dancing or going out like you used to."

"Mom! Would you listen to me?" Elena produced a small white stick from her pocket. "It says it's positive."

Gin took the stick. "It's a false positive, then, because it's impossible. If you haven't been with anyone in reality, then you can't be pregnant. You can't fake biology."

"But what if there was a way—somehow, through the sensor?"

Gin shook her head. "There would have to be delivery of sperm, somehow. You would have had to have ordered it from a donor company; it couldn't be done without your knowledge."

163

"I don't know."

"Well, we'll call in a doctor," Gin said carefully.

"I'm not crazy!"

"I didn't say you were. But I think you're spending too much time in unreality."

"You can't say that to me."

"All right. But it's different for you. It's changed in the last three months. Ever since—"

"Don't talk about it. I can't talk about it."

"Okay, I won't. But please, just think. Couldn't what happened have got into your mind, somehow, and translated into, into imagining a new life—your mind wanting to create something innocent and vulnerable?"

"Stop, please. You sound like Dr. Betty from the afternoon shows."

"Fine. Just try to think about how things have changed for you recently. You're not taking care of yourself the way you once did."

"Just let me think."

*　*　*

Elena left her mother and went back to her room, unsure why she had gone to Gin for help, because Gin was more deeply lost in the unreal world—or was she? Elena knew she was becoming the thing she feared becoming, and while she knew she had allowed it to happen, she felt helpless to stop it because in the past few months, the unreal world had surrounded her and absorbed her in so complete a way that she felt she belonged to it. There was safety in the distance. But there was a quality to the absorption that felt seductive and ominous, like beautiful dark storm clouds on a distant horizon that hadn't yet displayed lightning, or a flower whose pollen could kill. Her mind was remaking reality, and deep in her psyche she felt herself being thrown from the earth, spinning farther away from the world, like gravity had suddenly lost its power.

At the same time she had felt her body change, getting softer, her stomach expanding, yes, as she became sedentary, but it was also something more—a growing sense of loss coming from a place she couldn't name, something that needed replacement. She felt reality was slipping, that somehow flesh and blood had morphed with electronic energy and was creating a new kind of existence, and as the thought occurred to her, she felt a stirring from deep within her belly, under her not-quite-believing hand. Larus had become her guide in the unreality and she tethered herself to him like an anchor or a compass, and quite honestly, he was the most tender and caring lover she'd had, or didn't have. There were so many ways to love someone—who was she to say it wasn't *really* physical? The ultimate protected kind. Except it hadn't been. Things had gotten so confused in the last months, and Elena had felt so calm, in the unreality, floating on the aftereffects of the compound. Things changed so fast in the unreal world that maybe there was some way that it could have happened. Or maybe none of this was happening and she would wake up from the strange nightmare her life had become.

Reality exists only in our minds. We're each living in different ones.

She meant to call a doctor, but instead Elena found herself calling Larus.

He answered, appearing in her room as a blue ghost. Seeing a measure of seriousness in her face, he sat on the bed.

Elena took his hand, telling him her suspicions, with little preamble.

"Congratulations," Larus said, without irony or shock.

"But it can't be possible—right?"

"If you've been with someone in the past few months, it could be," he said. Absent from his voice was any anger, jealousy. No accusations.

"Larus," Elena said. "I've only been with you."

"Yes, and that was wonderful. But there must be another explanation."

"How could it have happened? Could your sperm have been conveyed to me, somehow?"

"No, that is impossible. Quite possibly you're experiencing a hysterical pregnancy, possibly an emotional reaction to witnessing the child being killed."

Hearing him say it so clinically sounded like bricks falling on a street. Just like her mother had suggested, just minutes before.

"How can you be so matter-of-fact? About any of it?" Elena shook her head.

"I'm sorry. Should I react another way?"

"Why do you seem different?" *Because he doesn't want to take responsibility*, she thought, but it felt like something more.

"I apologize. This is a highly unexpected development. I'm still working through my empathetic responsiveness."

Elena felt a hollow place spread in her viscera. "Why do you sound like an AI?"

He gave her a surprised look. "Surely, you understood when we met."

"Larus—what are you talking about?"

She stared at Larus's blue ghost, watching in horror as it faded from her view.

A message spun up from a tab, streaming across her white bedroom wall. It was addressed to her mother.

Congratulations, Virginia, the notification said. *You are among the first users to have experienced the Beta test of the Twelve-point-oh PALpablexity Sylph Artificial Intelligence Cybernetic Relationship Series. We are grateful for your user experience, and your biofeedback will be valuable in determining necessary debugging and improvements before presenting Twelve-point-oh to the public. Please accept a PALpablexity gift card and six free months of your very own Twelve-point-oh subscription. Proudly based in Los Angeles, connecting with the world.*

Elena's vision shadowed at the edges and her chest constricted before her mind had a chance to accept what had happened.

Larus didn't exist. The "pregnancy" was simply a response to the program.

Quickly, she requested *Larus* in a search engine.

Larus is a large genus of gulls with worldwide distribution.

A large cosmopolitan genus of gulls comprising many of the better-known gulls and being the type of the family Laridae.

A virtual ornithologist, named for a common bird. Destined for worldwide distribution.

Humans always become something else. Maybe that's what humanity is.

Elena rushed back to her mother's room, sharing the message.

"Did you sign up for this?"

Gin watched the words scroll on the wall, the dawning of something on her face. "I—I don't remember. I could have."

"The message was addressed to you!"

"They send me so many things."

"That's why he was older. He was meant for you, not me."

"This can't be happening."

"The system must have picked up our home signature; that's why he—it—started talking to me at the store."

"I'm sorry, Elena—this shouldn't have happened."

"How could you?"

"I didn't know this was what they were sending. I didn't intend for this to happen to you."

"Well, it *did* happen!" Elena gripped her stomach, feeling a terrible cramp. The next one brought her to her knees.

Gin stood.

"We're going to the hospital," she said, and Elena didn't argue as her mother lifted her from the floor and pulled her out the apartment, out the building and into the cycle repair shop.

One look at Elena told Ronnie what they needed, and he hurried Elena to one of his repaired bikes, one with a sidecar. Ronnie invited Gin to ride with him on the cycle.

"Just go," Gin said, and he did.

As they sped through the streets, Ronnie said, "I think St. Vincent's is closest."

Elena looked down and saw red spreading across the fabric of her pants.

* * *

They kept her for a few days, observation, they said, but Elena knew she was in the psych ward. At night Gin visited her, delivered by Ronnie, trembling under protective sunshield and gloves, and she sat with Elena for as long as they would let her.

After several hours, Elena finally took Gin's gloved hand.

"I'm so stupid," Elena said.

"We've all been stupid," Gin said.

Elena turned her head toward the wall, which displayed a lush, green forest, something perhaps from the Pacific Northwest. "Turn it off."

Gin fumbled for the control on Elena's bedside. The first button she hit changed the scene to a thin waterfall spilling into an emerald-colored pond. Then rolling hills with ropy-looking sheep. Finally she hit the correct button and the display went dark, leaving gray walls.

"That's better," Elena said, and closed her eyes.

* * *

When they released Elena, it was night, and her mother had gone home.

Instead of calling Ronnie for a ride, Elena wandered the city. She came upon a marketplace, reaching out absently to touch pistachios in a barrel, recalling the feeling of touching seeds while at home in her RRmask, trying to differentiate what she felt now from what she felt then.

A few blue ghosts of people—or perhaps generated, unreal people—walked by, laughing about something, and Elena sidestepped out of their way.

Her hand went to her flat belly, marveling at feeling an overwhelming sense of loss when there had been nothing there to begin with.

Was it like her mother had suggested, that her mind had generated the false life to make up for the ones that had been lost? She breathed the exhaust-and-smoke-and-garbage-laden air, let her ears absorb the sound of cycles zipping past her, the voices of people both real and not talking about topics both real and not. She absorbed the colors around her, the gray-brown of city walls and city streets, blackened fruit in the gutter, grimy but brightly colored umbrellas and awnings over shops and stands, barrels of green and orange vegetables, glowing advertisements in false windows, glowing people, false people, false relationships, dogs on leashes, paper fliers, clouds of humid mist, blinding streetlights, the black and quiet sky reaching to infinite spaces beyond. Was the real world safer for her psyche than the unreal one? Was the real world real?

She stood on the street feeling everything she could feel, turning her face upward to absorb the rays of a streetlight, crying quietly in the night air. She was in danger of someone taking her for sunsick, and maybe she was, maybe all the time spent in the false daylight had created a sort of false sickness the same way it had created a false pregnancy, or maybe now that she was out of the sun, she was really waking up for the first time.

Eventually, she heard a motorcycle stop near her.

"The hospital called your mother," Ronnie said. "They said you left."

Wordlessly, she slid onto the seat behind him, and he took her home.

* * *

Ronnie rolled the bike slowly through Phoung's, which was emptying out for the night, and parked the bike inside his repair shop.

"I just—need a minute before I go in."

He sat next to Elena on a bench near the restaurant entrance.

"Maybe I need a lot of minutes before I go in," Elena said.

She took his hand. It felt like when Larus took her hand, but warmer.

"Are you real?" Elena asked.

"As real as you are." He kissed her hand.

"I don't know what to do next. I don't know how to move forward."

"You go inside and sleep, and wake up tomorrow night."

"But what will things look like now?"

"They'll look more clear."

"I'm afraid," Elena said.

"You won't get lost again."

"How can you be so nice to me?"

"How can I not?" He kissed her forehead.

It felt real.

* * *

Elena took one of the pills they had given her at the hospital, not the compound, but something different. She slept, with fitful and restless dreams in which Larus appeared, paper-like and two-dimensional, his body wrinkling and tearing when Elena spilled a cup of coffee. She dreamed nightmares of burning piles of bones, of young men being dragged from motorcycles in the dead of night. She dreamed of other things she couldn't remember, except for images of buildings glowing blue like ghosts, or of fruit at the market disappearing in her hands, leaving her with a mournful hunger. She woke and stared at the white ceiling, not wanting to move, not wanting to be there, not wanting to be anywhere.

Who are we? She thought. *What are we doing here?*

When it was nearly dark, Elena pulled herself out of her bed and found her mother waiting at the kitchen table with a cup of tea. She stood to pour Elena one and set it in front of her.

"I'm weaning myself off the compound," Gin announced, her hands still trembling, and Elena realized that Gin had already started detoxing when she visited Elena in the hospital—she was shaking from withdrawal, not fear. "And I'm spending a little less time with my RRmask."

"Why now?"

"You know why," Gin said.

Elena looked at her hands, the flaws in her skin.

"Listen to me. You can't do this anymore. The way you felt, for the last few months—that wasn't you."

Gin stood, opened a drawer and pulled out a notebook and a pen.

"All I ever wanted was to keep you safe. I thought you'd be safe from danger in our apartment, but clearly that's not true."

On a blank page, Gin drew a small circle at the bottom and then a series of lines moving up the page. Gin wrote highway names and then street names and scratched an "X" at a point near the top of the page.

"Our family had a cabin," Gin said. "I don't know if it's still there, or if someone has moved in, but this is where it is. It's on a lake, and there are fish. There's room for a garden. There are, or there were, a few neighbors around. There were deer and rabbits and elk and moose. Before you leave, you should buy a gun—someone in the city can help you, right? There's got to be someone you know."

Elena watched her mother as if she were another figure in unreality, a dream. Her mother took Elena's hand and placed the illegible map into it.

"Go to Ronnie, buy one of the motorcycles. Better yet, see if he wants to go with you."

"Mom."

"More people like you are out there, trying to make a life as best they can. I've heard stories. They live together, out there, despite everything. It's dangerous but they have a life, a real life."

"Mom, stop."

Gin released her. "Pack a bag now," she said. "The sun is about to set."

* * *

After Elena retreated to her room, Gin stood at the apartment door with her fingers on the handle. A few times she started to open the door and stopped. It was easier when she had a reason, when Elena was in danger, like rushing to put out a fire.

Gin finally pulled the door open to a puff of stale air, motor oil and cooking food. She took a step, standing fully outside her apartment, feeling wobbly, like she was riding a train. She forced her feet to move, sliding one after the other, feeling naked without her layers of protective covering. She made it to the end of the hall, to the entrance of the bike shop. She trembled in the frame of the doorway until Ronnie noticed her.

"Gin," he said. He was holding a metal tool and set it on a workbench, grabbing a smudged towel. "Is everything okay?"

She looked at her feet. Ronnie took her hand and helped her descend a couple of steps, and she sat.

"I'm afraid for her."

Ronnie sat on the greasy step next to her.

"Can you help her?" Gin said. "Can you be there for her?"

"I want to be."

"Can you go? Would you leave the city?"

He gazed at the shop, at the two-wheeled vehicles in various states of unfinished brokenness.

"I might," he said. "Would she?"

"She has to."

"Would you?" Ronnie asked Gin.

"I think it's too late for me."

"Is it?"

"And I'm afraid it's too late for her."

They sat for a while, and when the sun set, the doors to the restaurant opened automatically, and beyond the restaurant, the exterior doors opened, ready to let people in for the night.

* * *

In her room, Elena stood motionless in front of her closet. One by one, she selected each item of clothing, touched the fabric, the buttons, zippers, collars. She examined the colors. She traced the curve of the hangers.

Were they real? Was the fabric, the cut, the style? She replaced each item and left the clothes in place, lined neatly in familiar places.

She reached a hand out and examined her skin, the delicate bones.

After a long time, she dimmed the lights and settled into her soft chair.

"Access PALpablexity gift card," Elena said, and slid the mask over her eyes.

ACKNOWLEDGMENTS

I love being a part of the whole magical, weird thing that is creativity.

I've been lucky enough to have had a bevy of talented writers share their time by reading one or more of the stories in this collection and offering their insight. They include Laurin Bellg, Kim Brown, Regina Caesar, Felicia Clark, Nancy Coleman, Steve Fox, Sarah Fuelleman, Robin Gaines, Danielle McClelland, Steve Polansky, Jess Riley, Emily Shearer, Jill Schmaedeke, Ellen Welcker, and Dulcie Witman.

Writing is a painstaking process and most things go through several drafts and then a few more, and then it goes to the editors and proofreaders, who still find ways to make a manuscript better. My sincerest thanks to Cornerstone Press, including Director & Publisher Dr. Ross K. Tangedal, editors Grace Dahl, Brett Hill, and Maria Scherer, and production director Amanda Leibham for the beautiful cover design.

Thank you to Jolly Goins for her fabulous creative work on my author website, nikkikallio.com.

Readers often want to know where writers get their ideas from. Sometimes the origins are difficult to trace, forming through a combination of random thoughts and questions that suddenly coalesce into an idea. "Geography Lesson," however, has a clear beginning: a book sale. I found the 1977 edition of Webster's *New Geographical Dictionary* one year at the annual fall sale held by the American Association of University Women in Appleton, Wisconsin, and was entranced by the book's collective descriptions of mountains, rivers and towns. I thought, what if this was all you had to explain what Earth was? And the story of Fiona and her dad was born. So, thank you, AAUW, for putting on that great book sale, and thank you to whoever donated that book.

Some of the stories were developed during the fabulous writing retreats of Wide Open Writing, including "The Last Day," which appears largely in the form that it first arrived, in a creative rush on a sun-warmed Tuscan hill near my favorite tree.

Finally, my gratitude goes to my dear parents, who set a great example early on with their love for reading and books. With my deepest love and admiration, thank you.

Gratefully acknowledged are the following publications, where particular stories appeared in different forms:

"Geography Lesson" and "Spirit Box" appeared in *Wisconsin People & Ideas*.

"Shadow" appeared in *Minerva Rising* and *Midwestern Gothic*.

"A Night-Blooming Flower" appeared in *Minerva Rising*.

"Missing Mary" appeared in *Pitkin Review*.

"Float" appeared in *rawboned*.

Several stories received citations from various publications and organizations prior to publication in this collection. Gratefully acknowledged are the following:

"Geography Lesson" is the winner of the 2014 Mill Prize for Fiction and the 2015 *Wisconsin People & Ideas* Fiction Contest.

"Shadow" was nominated for a Pushcart Prize by *Midwestern Gothic*.

"The Last Day" and an earlier version of "Disappearing" were longlisted in *Fractured Lit*'s 2020 Flash Fiction contest.

"A Night-Blooming Flower" received Honorable Mention as "When Flowers Bloom at Night" for the 2013 Lakefly Literary Conference Flash Fiction award.

"Spirit Box" received 2nd place in the 2019 *Wisconsin People & Ideas* Fiction Contest.

The first chapters of "The Fledgling" were shortlisted for the 2018 Brain Mill Press Unsolicited Novella Contest.

Nikki Kallio is an award-winning writer, editor, and educator. She received an MFA from Goddard College and has led workshops for events like the UntitledTown book and author festival and organizations including The Mill: A Place for Writers and Wide Open Writing. Her work has appeared in *Midwestern Gothic*, *Minerva Rising*, *Wisconsin People & Ideas*, and elsewhere. Her essay "Cold Front" appeared in the anthology *(Her)oics: Women's Lived Experiences During the Coronavirus Pandemic* (2021). She worked as a newspaper journalist on both coasts before coming home to Wisconsin, where she now resides.